Tales of Fear
&
Frightening Phenomena

Tales of Fear
&
Frightening
Phenomena

AN ANTHOLOGY BY

HELEN HOKE

LODESTAR BOOKS
E. P. DUTTON   NEW YORK

Copyright © 1982 by Helen Hoke

LIBRARY OF CONGRESS CATALOGING IN PUBLICATION DATA

Main entry under title:
Tales of fear and frightening phenomena.
    "Lodestar books."
    Contents: Love me, love me, love me / M. S. Waddell— Most dangerous game / Richard Connell— Return to the sabbath / Robert Bloch— The amorous ghost / Enid Bagnold— [etc.]
    1. Horror tales, English. 2. Horror tales, American. 3. Children's stories, English.
4. Children's stories, American. [1. Horror— Fiction. 2. Short stories] I. Hoke, Helen, date.
PZ5.T255   1982   823'.0876'08   [Fic]   82-7299
ISBN 0—525—66789—X   AACR2

Published in the United States by E. P. Dutton, Inc., 2 Park Avenue, New York, N.Y. 10016
Published simultaneously in Canada by Clarke, Irwin & Company Limited, Toronto and Vancouver
Editor: Virginia Buckley   Designer: Trish Parcell
Printed in the U.S.A.   First Edition
10 9 8 7 6 5 4 3 2 1

ACKNOWLEDGMENTS

The selections in this book are used by permission of and special arrangements with the proprietors of their respective copyrights, who are listed below. The editor's and publisher's thanks go to all who have made this collection possible.

The editor and publisher have made every effort to trace ownership of all material contained herein. It is their belief that the necessary permissions from the publishers, authors, and authorized agents have been obtained in all cases. In the event of any questions arising as to the use of any material, the editor and publisher express regret for any error unconsciously made and will be pleased to make the necessary corrections in future editions of the book.

"The Amorous Ghost," by Enid Bagnold, from *The Ghost Book,* edited by Cynthia Asquith, published by James Barrie (Hutchinson Publishing Group).

"Fear," by P. C. Wren. Reprinted by permission of John Murray (Publishers) Ltd.

"Love Me, Love Me, Love Me," by M. S. Waddell. Reprinted by permission of the author.

"Return to the Sabbath," by Robert Bloch. Reprinted by permission of the author and his agents, the Scott Meredith Literary Agency Inc., 845 Third Avenue, New York, NY 10022, U.S.A.

"Tarnhelm, or the Death of My Uncle Robert," by Sir Hugh Seymour Walpole. Reprinted by permission of Sir Rupert Hart-Davis.

"The Turn of the Tide," by C. S. Forester. Copyright © 1934, 1961 by C. S. Forester. Reprinted by permission of the Harold Matson Company, Inc. and A. D. Peters & Co., Ltd.

"The Whole Town's Sleeping," by Ray Bradbury. Copyright © 1950 by Ray Bradbury, © renewed 1978 by Ray Bradbury. Reprinted by permission of the Harold Matson Company, Inc.

for my son, John Hoke

Contents

About This Book

FEAR TRIGGERS A DISQUIETING ANTICIPATION of some expected evil. An imminent or unexpected danger, be it actual or imaginary, excites alarm. In *Tales of Fear and Frightening Phenomena,* an endeavor has been made to present stories that embody the essence of fear. To this end, the "goosefleshers" chosen are written by masterful writers. The much-admired novelist and playwright Enid Bagnold is included. Her short, but engaging, contribution to this book may pleasantly surprise those readers to whom she is known only through her longer works. Ray Bradbury, a natural choice for an anthology of this kind, C. S. Forester, and Sir Hugh Seymour Walpole are three more fine authors whose works were selected to fit the bill of fear proposed here.

The frightful phenomena in "Fear" by P. C. Wren occur in a remote spot in the jungles of the Far East. An isolated, abandoned bungalow is sought out by a traveler whose aim is to escape the fanfare of our mundane and hectic way of life. Jungle swamps, infested with myriads of dangers from tropical disease to poisonous creepers and crawlers, are nothing to the spirit of this adventurer. Here is a story to set the imagination on fire and cause the blood to run cold at the same time, particularly when you find out how he comes to know *real* fear.

Enid Bagnold's story, "The Amorous Ghost," is set in a comfortable, bourgeois house in the suburbs where all is run like a clock until "an upset," as the butler put it, takes place. Your sympathy will probably be with the master of the house, once you discover why he felt cold fear wandering down his spine.

In Robert Bloch's "Return to the Sabbath," two Hollywood executives decide to hire a leading actor who instills ghastly reality into the foreign horror movie he is appearing in. The frightful overlapping of the real and the unreal that follows in this unusually disquieting tale may well cause sweat to crystallize into icy drops.

In Ray Bradbury's superb story, recent strangulations of innocent victims by a maniac set the people of a small American town on edge. But, according to the criminal's pattern of behavior, his next murder is a whole month away. In the meantime, "The Whole Town's Sleeping."

So steel yourselves.

The rest of the stories in this book, involving other terrifying situations or extraordinary phenomena, are equally gripping. In one of these you will witness a life-and-death duel between unequal adversaries, while in another you will puzzle over an inexplicable metamorphosis of the ghastliest sort. We have all been taught that crime does not pay, but you will be horrified when you discover in yet another chiller exactly *why* a particular crime proved so disastrous.

It is hoped you will receive and enjoy telepathic shocks from every story. The tales were chosen, after all, for exactly this reason: your reading pleasure.

Helen Hoke

Love Me,
Love Me, Love Me

M. S. WADDELL

I WAS NOT ALONE.

I stopped and turned around. I knew there was somebody there, somebody following, somebody who did not want to be seen, somebody shy.

Well, all right, so there was nobody there. Maybe it was just my imagination . . . again.

I lit a cigarette, pausing beneath a streetlamp. Maybe it was nerves, maybe I had been doing too much, maybe now was the time to do something about it. I'm not made of iron. Time to take a rest. I walked on up the avenue, mechanically counting my paces between the trees that flanked it.

Harcourt could do it . . . no doubt about that. He was able, he knew the ropes. Nothing would go far wrong with Harcourt in charge. There was no need to actually go away. I could stay at home . . . where I would be on hand if anything happened.

The feeling again, the feeling that somebody was watching me. I fought against it, unavailingly. I turned around.

[3]

Nothing.

A quiet road, trees, and bushes, an odd friendly light winking over the top of a hedge, only not so many now as there usually were because now it was getting late, or early, depending on the way you look at it. One thirty A.M., a cool morning, not unpleasant. The way I like it . . . the best way for relaxing: not lying in bed, getting up and walking. Not far, just along the road and back, makes the thoughts stand still, makes things insignificant. People, too many people all day . . . nobody at night . . . usually.

So I quickened my pace. Maybe it would be better to get home, get to bed. This feeling . . . this was bad. Feet on the ground . . . people with feet on the ground don't start imagining things, not this way . . . this rustling on the road behind me.

Turn around . . . again? All right . . . *don't* turn around. So what about the rustling on the road . . . a dog?

Glad to get home just the same. I unlatched the gate, turned up the path. Thirty yards, feet scraping on the gravel. Keys . . . groping for the keys, fumbling for the lock.

Someone was standing at the gate, something. A shape . . . colorless . . . then it was gone, faded. Imagination . . . or not imagination? I went back down to the gate. Nothing. Always nothing.

Or was there? Nothing tangible . . . but there was something. A feeling in the air . . . a fondness . . . the only way to describe it. Something personal about the night.

Then there wasn't. There was only night, impersonal. Time to go inside, to go to bed. To fix it with Harcourt tomorrow for a rest . . . a real rest.

Back into the house . . . a drink . . . to calm things down.

Looking through the window . . . there is nothing at the gate.

There is nothing at the gate.

There *is* something at the gate . . . someone. A someone . . .
waiting at the gate. Last night . . . I don't know about last
night. Maybe there wasn't last night. Tonight there *is* someone,
or something—I don't know—at the gate. Curiously, there is no
feeling of anxiety about it in my mind . . . curiosity, yes . . .
that much good the day's rest has done.

This thing at the gate. . . . It still isn't there when I look
directly. Just now and then . . . a glance through the curtains
and there it is, glowing faintly in the light from the road.

Harcourt is coming tonight. That ought to be for the best. I
can see clearly now . . . inside the gate. Never close . . . but
inside the gate standing at the foot of the garden in the darkness.

It's not so shy now . . . it lets me look at it. I'm not afraid.
Maybe it is imagination . . . maybe not. If not, then I should be
afraid. But I'm not . . . just rather happy. I'm not afraid . . .
maybe *it* is, or shy or something.

Harcourt didn't see it. It was near to him, close to him in the
darkness, but he didn't know. I didn't ask him. I couldn't ask
him because he would have thought . . . well, it's obvious what
he would have thought. . . . Wouldn't anybody?

You can't talk to a man like Harcourt about a thing like . . .
the thing. Can you call a thing a person? Harcourt has his head
firmly screwed on. You can talk to him about budgets and
schedules and items for procedure . . . my sort of man, a man
who doesn't need an imagination.

We talked. We sat by the window and talked. I kept the
curtains back. . . . I wanted to see if he would see it. I didn't
want him to see it . . . not really. If he saw it, then it wasn't an
it . . . it was something that could be classified and boxed away
in his orderly mind. . . . If he didn't see it, it was part of my
imagination, or strain from overwork or nerves.

Well . . . he didn't see it.

It saw *him.*

[5]

He must have seen it, if it was there to see. It came right out into the light as it has never done before, right up the garden towards the window.

I know more about it now. It looks like a woman . . . a girl, not a woman. Too slight for a woman, too soft in its movements. It never actually seems to move. One minute it is in one spot, the next a little farther on. But coming towards the house, definitely. White . . . or perhaps not really white. Colorless, like water formed into a shape, like rain frozen into a pattern on glass.

"You know your way?" I asked Harcourt at the door.

"Down to the station . . . yes."

I held the door open for him.

"Good night."

"Good night."

He walked down the path.

I stood in the door. He must have thought I was watching him particularly, he made a gesture of farewell at the gate.

The thing was standing against the hedge. It had the most wistful, sad little face I have ever seen. It stood as high as my shoulder, still, more than is implied by still . . . motionless, its fingers clasped against its cape. It had turned its face aside so that I could not look directly upon it. It wore high old-fashioned shoes, a long, plain-cut dress, a cape draped over its shoulders.

I waited at the door. It did not move.

"Come in," I said out loud. "You can come in."

I stepped forward, and it was gone.

"You mustn't be afraid of me," I said, standing in the garden in the darkness. "You mustn't be afraid." My voice sounded shrill, uncertain. I was trying to be sincere. It was afraid, and cold and lost, wherever it was, wherever it had been.

I waited a minute, two, three . . . till there was no point in it. I turned back to the house, pausing at the door. "You don't have to be afraid of me," I said again, softly.

I went back into the sitting-room. I sat by the window, looking out, in my favorite chair, where it would expect to see me. I waited. I went to sleep.

Morning . . . and the sun shining through the glass. I awoke slowly, comfortable, taking my time like a tabby cat. Plenty of time . . . all the time in the world.

Only it was running short of time . . . it had not found what it needed, it was still searching, with all the time in the world, but short of time.

In the moisture on the windowpane it had traced with its finger, "Love me, Love me, Love me."

Tonight Harcourt walked through it. It was waiting by the door when I let him in, and he moved through it. Just for a moment its face mingled with Harcourt's smart black suit, then I was looking at it over his shoulder . . . and it was looking at me.

"You look pale," Harcourt said, as I closed the door. "You were right to take a rest."

"I don't know," I said. "I'm beginning to wonder if it *was* such a good idea."

"Oh?"

I looked at his face. He wasn't really interested. Fair enough . . . he wasn't paid to be interested.

"Gets a bit lonely out here," I said. "You know the way it is."

"Go off somewhere then," he said, settling in his chair by the table, spreading the papers from his briefcase before him. "Nothing to hold you here, is there?"

"No," I said. "I suppose not."

We went on to other things then . . . Harcourt's sort of things. But I went on thinking about it . . . and it wasn't right. There *was* something to hold me here . . . there was that thing in the garden for a start.

Just how long was it going to stay in the garden?

Not long. She was waiting in the hall when I showed Harcourt to the door. The same frozen stance, the same fragile hand clutching the edge of her cape.

I let Harcourt out, closed the door, turned around. She was still there, standing at the foot of the stairs, her eyes upon me.

"Well, you're in at last," I said. "What do you want?"

For a wraith she wasn't very forthcoming. Just the eyes, soft and sad, trying to say something. A fragile little thing.

"I don't know how to get through to you," I said. "I'm sorry, I don't know what you want."

She smiled. It was the first time I had actually seen her make any movement. It was a nice smile, wistful maybe, but nice. Then she started to fade. One minute she was standing against the banister, the next she wasn't.

"You mustn't be afraid," I said, hopefully.

There wasn't much point in waiting about in the hall for a timid spectre, so I abandoned the idea. Maybe she couldn't stay in one place very long? She was gone, anyway.

I waited around a bit that night, just to see if she would put in an appearance. Nothing happened. Once or twice there seemed to be a shade, a movement in the firelight, but she didn't let me see her.

So it went on for a day or two. She would turn up at odd spots around the house, just standing there, smiling. Once she reached out towards me, dainty fingers uncoiling. I moved towards her . . . too quickly . . . she faded away. That was the way it always was . . . she *wanted* me . . . she wanted to contact me, to try me, but she was afraid.

Harcourt still came each night. She didn't pay any attention to him. Once or twice she appeared in the room while we were talking, once standing by the window, frowning, again seated in the large leather armchair, her hands folded coyly in her lap. She was watching me, all the time, so that it was *hard* to keep my mind on what Harcourt was saying.

"This can't go on," I said one night, after Harcourt had left. She was still there in the armchair, still smiling. "We're not getting anywhere."

I came towards her, slowly this time, so as not to scare her. I had learned my lesson. I stopped, two or three feet from the chair. I extended my hand.

"It's all right," I said. "All right."

She pushed away from my hand, so that, just for a moment, her body faded into the back of the armchair . . . but she was learning too, she did not fade away.

"It's all right. You're all right," I went on saying.

Then her hand stretched out and touched my right shoulder. A shock of cold ran down my arm. A withering, stinging sensation. I snatched my hand back, involuntarily. She faded away. I was left clutching my right arm, my cold arm, with my left hand.

That was the beginning . . . the real beginning, I suppose. For the first time I was afraid. I was afraid because I wanted to touch her, I wanted to stroke that face, to hold that tiny chill hand. I knew *she* knew it. . . . I knew that was what she wanted . . . that the other, the talking, the searching for communication had all been to her the byplay of love. This was what she had come for, this was the meaning of the words she had traced on the window, "Love me, Love me, Love me."

It was easy. There was no one to come between us. Harcourt came, but he came only at night and he did not stay for long. She came to me . . . she came at odd times, there was no rhyme or reason. She came, and she would sit there smiling, and I would come to her and reach out and take her in my arms and press her cold little nothingness of a body to mine, and the chill would run through me.

"You don't look well," Harcourt said, gathering his papers together. For once there was a note of genuine concern in his voice.

[9]

"I feel well enough in the circumstances."

"Your accident, of course." His voice trailed off. He was looking at my arm, the white edges of bandage that showed beneath my sleeve.

"A scald," I said, "rather more severe than I thought."

"You've had a doctor, of course."

"Of course."

He believed me. He has been trained to believe me and not to question.

Then he left. I went back into the room and she was standing by the window, watching him go. But she turned to me again, and I came to her, and the short sharp chill ran down the side of my face as her formless fingers stretched out to me.

She touches me now, strokes me. I know that where she strokes me the flesh will wither and peel, the tissue will rot, the blood will dry. She strokes me now. I cannot draw myself from her because I love her, but soon . . . soon it will be over.

Harcourt came again tonight. He let himself in. . . . I have given him a key. He came up to the bedroom and we talked. I kept the room dark so that he could not see . . . what there was to see. I told him it was my eyes . . . but he will know soon enough.

She was watching. She sat at the foot of the bed and watched him. Once or twice I saw his eyes flicker towards the place where she sat as though he saw something, a half shape in the darkness. But then he has a rational mind.

He said good-bye and he got up to leave. She stirred. He went out. She stood at the foot of the bed. She smiled at me, and she turned her head away and glided from the room and I knew that she was going, too.

I watch them from the window. He strides down the road, she glides behind him. He turns suddenly, as though he senses something there. He stops. He lights a cigarette. He shakes his head, he walks on.

A scrap of withered flesh falls from my face onto the carpet as I turn, to grope my way back to the bed.

She was mine . . . she was *mine* . . . !

Most Dangerous Game

RICHARD CONNELL

THERE WAS NO SOUND in the night as Rainsford sat there but the muffled throb of the engine that drove the yacht swiftly through the darkness, and the swish and ripple of the wash of the propeller. Rainsford, reclining in a steamer chair, indolently puffed on his favorite briar. "It's so dark," he thought, "that I could sleep without closing my eyes; the night would be my eyelids—"

An abrupt sound startled him. Off to the right he heard it and his ears, expert in such matters, could not be mistaken. Again he heard the sound, and again. Somewhere, off in the blackness, someone had fired a gun three times. Rainsford sprang up and moved quickly to the rail, mystified. He strained his eyes in the direction from which the reports had come, but it was like trying to see through a blanket. He leaped upon the rail and balanced himself there, to get greater elevation; his pipe, striking a rope, was knocked from his mouth. He lunged for it; a short, hoarse cry came from his lips as he realized he had reached too far and had lost his balance. The cry was pinched off short as the blood-warm waters of the Caribbean Sea closed over his head.

He struggled up to the surface and tried to cry out, but the wash from the speeding yacht slapped him in the face and the saltwater in his open mouth made him gag and strangle. Desperately he struck out with strong strokes after the receding lights of the yacht, but he stopped before he had swum fifty feet. A certain coolheadedness had come to him; it was not the first time he had been in a tight place. There was a chance that his cries could be heard by someone aboard the yacht, but that chance was slender and grew more slender as the yacht raced on. He wrestled himself out of his clothes and shouted with all his power. The lights of the yacht became faint and ever-vanishing fireflies; then they were blotted out entirely by the night.

Rainsford remembered the shots. They had come from the right, and doggedly he swam in that direction, swimming with slow, deliberate strokes, conserving his strength. For a seemingly endless time he fought the sea. He began to count his strokes; he could do possibly a hundred more, he thought, and then—

Rainsford heard a sound. It came out of the darkness, a high, screaming sound, the sound of an animal in an extremity of anguish and terror. He did not recognize the animal that made the sound, he did not try to; with fresh vitality he swam towards the sound. He heard it again, then it was cut short by another noise, crisp, staccato.

"Pistol shot," muttered Rainsford, swimming on.

Ten minutes of determined effort brought another sound to his ears—the most welcome he had ever heard—the muttering and growling of the sea breaking on a rocky shore. He was almost on the rocks before he saw them; on a night less calm he would have been shattered against them. With his remaining strength he dragged himself from the swirling waters. Gasping, his hands raw, he reached a flat piece at the top. Dense jungle came down to the very edge of the cliffs. What perils that tangle of trees and underbrush might hold for him did not concern Rainsford just then. All he knew was that he was safe from the enemy, the sea, and that utter weariness was on him. He flung himself down at the jungle edge and tumbled headlong into the deepest sleep of his life.

When he opened his eyes he knew from the position of the sun that it was late in the afternoon. Sleep had given him new vigor; a sharp hunger was picking at him. He looked about him, almost cheerfully.

Where there are pistol shots there are men; where there are men there is food, he thought. But what *kind* of men, he wondered, in so forbidding a place? An unbroken front of snarled and ragged jungle fringed the shore.

He saw no sign of a trail through the closely knit web of weeds and trees; it was easier to go along the shore, and Rainsford floundered along by the water. Not far from where he had landed, he stopped. Some wounded thing, by the evidence a large animal, had thrashed about in the underbrush; the jungle weeds were crushed down and the moss was lacerated; one patch of weeds was stained crimson. A small, glittering object not far away caught Rainsford's eye and he picked it up. It was an empty cartridge.

"A twenty-two," he remarked. "That's odd. It must have been a fairly large animal, too. The hunter had his nerve with him to tackle it with a light gun. It's clear that the brute put up a fight."

He examined the ground closely and found what he had hoped to find—the print of hunting boots. They pointed along the cliff in the direction he had been going. Eagerly he hurried along, now slipping on a rotten log or a loose stone, but making headway; night was beginning to settle down on the island.

Bleak darkness was blacking out the sea and jungle when Rainsford sighted the lights. He came upon them as he turned a crook in the coastline, and his first thought was that he had come upon a village, for there were many lights. But as he forged his way along he saw to his astonishment that all the lights were in one enormous building—a lofty structure with pointed towers plunging upwards into the gloom. His eyes made out the shadowy outlines of a palatial château; it was set on a high bluff and on three sides of it cliffs dived down to where the sea licked greedy lips in the shadows.

"Mirage," thought Rainsford. But it was no mirage, he found, when he opened the tall spiked iron gate. The stone steps were real enough, the massive door with a leering gargoyle for a knocker was real enough, yet about it all hung an air of unreality. He lifted the knocker and it creaked up stiffly as if it had never been used before. He thought he heard steps within, but the door remained closed. Again, Rainsford lifted the heavy knocker and let it fall. The door opened then, opened as suddenly as if it were on a spring, and Rainsford stood blinking in the river of glaring gold light that poured out. The first thing his eyes discerned was the largest man Rainsford had ever seen—a gigantic creature, solidly made and black-bearded to the waist. In his hand the man held a long-barrelled revolver and he was pointing it straight at Rainsford's heart. Out of the snarl of beard two small eyes regarded Rainsford.

"Don't be alarmed," said Rainsford, with a smile which he hoped was disarming. "I'm no robber. I fell off a yacht. My name is Sanger Rainsford of New York City."

The menacing look in the eyes did not change. The revolver pointed as rigidly as if the giant were a statue. He gave no sign that he understood Rainsford's words, or that he had even heard them. He was dressed in uniform, a black uniform trimmed with gray astrakhan.

"I'm Sanger Rainsford of New York," Rainsford began again. "I fell off a yacht. I am hungry."

The man's only answer was to raise with his thumb the hammer of his revolver. Then Rainsford saw the man's free hand go to his forehead in a military salute, and he saw him click his heels together and stand at attention. Another man was coming down the broad marble steps, an erect, slender man in evening clothes. He advanced to Rainsford and held out his hand. In a cultivated voice marked by a slight accent that gave it added precision and deliberateness, he said: "It is a very great pleasure and honor to welcome Mr. Sanger Rainsford, the celebrated hunter, to my home. I've read your book about hunting snow leopards in Tibet, you see," explained the man. "I am General Zaroff."

Rainsford's first impression was that the man was singularly handsome; his second was that there was an original, almost bizarre quality about the general's face. He was a tall man past middle age, for his hair was a vivid white, but his thick eyebrows and pointed military moustache were as black as the night from which Rainsford had come. His eyes, too, were black and very bright. He had high cheekbones, a sharp-cut nose, a spare, dark face, the face of a man used to giving orders, the face of an aristocrat. Turning to the giant in uniform, the general made a sign. The giant put away his pistol, saluted, withdrew.

"Ivan is an incredibly strong fellow," remarked the general, "but he has the misfortune to be deaf and dumb. A simple fellow, but, I'm afraid, like all his race, a bit of a savage."

"Is he Russian?"

"He is a Cossack," said the general, and his smile showed red lips and pointed teeth. "So am I."

"Come," he said, "we shouldn't be chatting here. We can talk later. Now you want clothes, food, rest. You shall have them. This is a most restful spot. Follow Ivan, if you please, Mr. Rainsford. I was about to have my dinner when you came. I'll wait for you. You'll find that my clothes will fit you, I think."

It was to a huge beam-ceiling bedroom with a canopied bed big enough for six men that Rainsford followed the silent giant. Ivan laid out an evening suit and Rainsford, as he put it on, noticed that it came from a London tailor who ordinarily cut and sewed for none below the rank of duke.

The dining room to which Ivan conducted him was in many

ways remarkable. It suggested a baronial hall of feudal times with its oaken panels, its high ceiling, its vast refectory table where two score men could sit down to eat. About the hall were the mounted heads of many animals—lions, tigers, elephants, moose, bears; larger or more perfect specimens Rainsford had never seen. The table appointments were of the finest—the linen, the crystal, the silver, the china.

Half apologetically, General Zaroff said: "We do our best to preserve the amenities of civilization here. Please forgive any lapses. We are well off the beaten track, you know."

The general seemed a most thoughtful and affable host, a true cosmopolite. But whenever he looked up from his plate, Rainsford found the general studying him, appraising him narrowly.

"Perhaps," said General Zaroff, "you were surprised that I recognized your name. You see, I read all books on hunting published in English, French, and Russian. I have but one passion in my life, Mr. Rainsford, and it is the hunt."

"You have some wonderful heads here," said Rainsford. "That Cape buffalo is the largest I ever saw. I've always thought that the Cape buffalo is the most dangerous of all big game."

For a moment the general did not reply; he was smiling his curious red-lipped smile. Then he said slowly: "No. You are wrong, sir. The Cape buffalo is not the most dangerous big game." He sipped his wine. "Here in my preserve on this island," he said, in the same slow tone, "I hunt more dangerous game."

Rainsford expressed his surprise. "Is there big game on this island?"

"Oh, it isn't here naturally, of course, I have to stock the island."

"What have you imported, General?" Rainsford asked. "Tigers?"

The general smiled. "No," he said. "Hunting tigers ceased to interest me some years ago. No thrill left in tigers, no real danger. I live for danger, Mr. Rainsford. We will have some capital hunting, you and I. I shall be most glad to have your society."

"But what game—" began Rainsford.

"I'll tell you," said the general. "You will be amused, I know. I think I may say, in all modesty, that I have done a rare thing. I have invented a new sensation."

The general continued: "God made some men poets. Some He makes kings, some beggars. Me, He made a hunter. My hand was made for the trigger, my father said. When I was only five years old he gave me a little gun, especially made in Moscow for me, to shoot sparrows with. I killed my first bear when I was ten. My whole life has been one prolonged hunt. I went into the army and for a time commanded a division of Cossack cavalry, but my real interest was always the hunt. I have hunted every kind of game in every land. It would be impossible for me to tell you how many animals I have killed.

"After the debacle in Russia I left the country; for it was imprudent for an officer of the Tsar to stay there. Luckily, I had invested heavily in American securities, so I shall never have to open a tearoom in Monte Carlo or drive a taxi in Paris. Naturally, I continued to hunt—grizzlies in your Rockies, crocodiles in the Ganges, rhinoceroses in East Africa. I went to the Amazon to hunt jaguars, for I had heard that they were unusually cunning. They weren't." The Cossack sighed. "They were no match at all for a hunter with his wits about him, and a high-powered rifle. I was bitterly disappointed.

"I was lying in my tent with a splitting headache one night when a terrible thought pushed its way into my mind. Hunting was beginning to bore me! And hunting, remember, had been my life. I asked myself why the hunt no longer fascinated me. You are much younger than I am, Mr. Rainsford, and have not hunted as much, but you perhaps can guess the answer."

"What was it?"

"Simply this: Hunting had ceased to be what you call a sporting proposition. It had become too easy. I always got my quarry. Always. There is no greater bore than perfection."

The general lit a fresh cigarette. "No animal had a chance with me anymore. That is no boast, it is a mathematical certainty. The animal had nothing but his legs and his instinct. Instinct is no match for reason. When I thought of this, it was a tragic moment for me, I tell you."

Rainsford leaned across the table, absorbed in what his host was saying.

"It came to me as an inspiration what I must do," the general went on.

"And that was?"

The general smiled the quiet smile of one who has faced an obstacle and surmounted it with success. "I had to invent a new animal to hunt," he said.

"A new animal? You're joking."

"Not at all," said the general. "I never joke about hunting. I bought this island, built this house, and here I do my hunting. The island is perfect for my purpose—there are jungles with a mass of trails in them, hills, swamps—"

"But the animal, General Zaroff?"

"Oh," said the general, "it supplies me with the most exciting hunting in the world. Every day I hunt, and I never grow bored now, for I have a quarry with which I can match my wits."

Rainsford's bewilderment showed in his face.

"I wanted the ideal animal to hunt," explained the general. "So I said: 'What are the attributes of an ideal quarry?' And the answer was, of course: 'It must have courage, cunning, and above all, it must be able to reason.'"

"But no animal can reason," objected Rainsford.

"My dear fellow," said the general, "there is one that can."

"But you can't mean—" gasped Rainsford.

"And why not?"

"I can't believe you are serious, General Zaroff. This is a grisly joke."

"Why should I not be serious? I am speaking of hunting."

"Hunting? Good God, General Zaroff, what you speak of is murder."

The general laughed. He regarded Rainsford quizzically. "I refuse to believe that so modern a man harbors romantic ideas about the value of human life. Surely your experiences in the war—"

"Did not make me condone cold-blooded murder," finished Rainsford, stiffly.

Laughter shook the general. "How extraordinarily droll you are!" he said. "One does not expect nowadays to find a young man of the educated class, even in America, with such a naive and, if I may say so, mid-Victorian point of view. It's like finding a snuffbox in a limousine. I'll wager you'll forget your notions when you go hunting with me. You've a genuine new thrill in store for you, Mr. Rainsford."

"Thank you, I'm a hunter, not a murderer."

"Dear me," said the general, quite unruffled, "again that unpleasant word. But I think I can show you that your scruples are quite ill-founded."

"Yes?"

"Life is for the strong, to be lived by the strong, and if needs be, taken by the strong. The weak of the world were put here to give the strong pleasure. I am strong. Why should I not use my gift? If I wish to hunt, why should I not? I hunt the scum of the earth—sailors from tramp ships—lascars, blacks, Chinese, whites, mongrels—a thoroughbred horse or hound is worth more than a score of them."

"But where do you get them?"

"This island is called Ship Trap," he answered. "Sometimes an angry god of the high seas sends them to me. Sometimes, when Providence is not so kind, I help Providence a bit. Come to the window with me.

"Watch! Out there!" exclaimed the general, pointing into the night. As the general pressed a button, far out to sea Rainsford saw the flash of lights.

The general chuckled. "They indicate a channel," he said, "where there's none: Giant rocks with razor edges crouch like a sea monster with wide-open paws. They can crush a ship as easily as I crush this nut." He dropped a walnut on the hardwood floor and brought his heel grinding down on it. "Oh, yes," he said, casually, as if in answer to a question, "I have electricity. We try to be civilized here."

"Civilized? And you shoot down men?"

A trace of anger was in the general's black eyes, but it was there for but a second, and he said, his his most pleasant manner: "Dear me, what a righteous young man you are! That would be barbarous. I treat these visitors with every consideration. They get plenty of good food and exercise. They get into splendid physical condition. You shall see for yourself tomorrow."

"What do you mean?"

"We'll visit my training school," smiled the general. "It's in the cellar. I have about a dozen pupils down there now. They're from the Spanish bark *Sanlucar* that had the bad luck to go on the rocks out there. A very inferior lot, I regret to say. Poor specimens and more accustomed to the deck than to the jungle."

He raised his hand, and Ivan brought thick Turkish coffee. Rainsford, with an effort, held his tongue in check.

"It's a game, you see," pursued the general, blandly. "I suggest to one of them that we go hunting. I give him a supply of food and an excellent hunting knife. I give him three hours' start. I am to follow, armed only with a pistol of the smallest caliber and range. If my quarry eludes me for three whole days, he wins the game. If I find him"—the general smiled—"he loses."

"Suppose he refuses to be hunted?"

"Oh," said the general, "I give him his option, of course. If he does not wish to hunt, I turn him over to Ivan. Ivan once had the honor of serving as official knouter to the Great White Tsar, and he has his own ideas of sport. Invariably, Mr. Rainsford, invariably they choose the hunt."

"And if they win?"

The smile on the general's face widened. "To date I have not lost," he said. Then he added, hastily, "I don't wish you to think me a braggart, Mr. Rainsford. Many of them afford the most elementary sort of problem. Occasionally I strike a tartar. One almost did win. I eventually had to use the dogs."

The general steered Rainsford to a window. The lights from the windows sent a flickering illumination that made grotesque patterns on the courtyard below, and Rainsford could see moving about there a dozen or so huge black shapes; as they turned towards him, their eyes glittered greenly.

"A rather good lot, I think," observed the general. "They are let out at seven every night. If anyone should try to get into my house—or out of it—something extremely regrettable would occur to him." He hummed a snatch of song.

"And now," said the general, "I want to show you my new collection of heads. Will you come with me to the library?"

"I hope," said Rainsford, "that you will excuse me tonight, General. I'm really not feeling at all well."

"Ah, indeed?" the general inquired solicitously. "Well, I suppose that's only natural, after your long swim. Tomorrow, you'll feel like a new man, I'll wager. Then we'll hunt, eh? I've one rather promising prospect—"

Rainsford was hurrying from the room.

"Sorry you can't go with me tonight," called the general. "I expect rather fair sport—a big, strong black. He looks resourceful—Well, good night, Mr. Rainsford, I hope you have a good night's rest."

The bed was good and the pyjamas of the softest silk, and he was tired in every fiber of his being, but nevertheless Rainsford could not quiet his brain with the opiate of sleep. He lay, eyes wide open. Once he thought he heard stealthy steps in the corridor outside his room. He sought to throw open the door, but it would not open. He went to the window and looked out. His room was high up in one of the towers. The lights of the château were out now and it was dark and silent, but there was a fragment of sallow moon and by its light he could see, dimly, the courtyard; there, weaving in and out in the pattern of shadow, were black, noiseless forms; the hounds heard him at the window and looked up expectantly with their green eyes. Rainsford went back to the bed and lay down. He had achieved a doze when, just as morning began to come, he heard, far off in the jungle, the faint report of a pistol.

General Zaroff did not appear until luncheon. He was dressed faultlessly in the tweeds of a country squire. He was solicitous about the state of Rainsford's health.

"As for me," sighed the general, "I do not feel as well. I am worried, Mr. Rainsford. Last night I detected traces of my old complaint. The hunting was not good last night. The fellow lost his head. He made a straight trail that offered no problems at all. That's the trouble with these sailors, they have dull brains to begin with and they do not know how to get about in the woods. It's most annoying."

"General," said Rainsford firmly, "I wish to leave this island at once."

The general raised his thickets of eyebrows; he seemed hurt. "But, my dear fellow," the general protested, "you've only just come. You've had no hunting—"

"I wish to go today," said Rainsford. He saw the dead black eyes of the general on him, studying him. General Zaroff's face suddenly brightened.

"Tonight," said the general, "we will hunt—you and I."

Rainsford shook his head. "No, General," he said, "I will not hunt."

The general shrugged his shoulders. "As you wish, my friend," he said. "The choice rests entirely with you. But may I venture to suggest that you will find my idea of sport more diverting than Ivan's!"

"You don't mean——" cried Rainsford.

"My dear fellow," said the general, "have I not told you I always mean what I say about hunting? This is really an inspiration. I drink to a foeman worthy of my steel—at last."

The general raised his glass, but Rainsford sat staring at him.

"You'll find this game worth playing," the general said, enthusiastically. "Your brain against mine. Your woodcraft against mine. Your strength and stamina against mine. And the stake is not without value, eh?"

"And if I win——" began Rainsford huskily.

"I'll cheerfully acknowledge myself defeated if I do not find you by midnight of the third day," said General Zaroff. "My sloop will place you on the mainland near a town. I will give you my word as a gentleman and a sportsman. Of course, you, in turn, must agree to say nothing of your visit here."

"I'll agree to nothing of the kind," said Rainsford.

"Oh," said the general, "in that case—but why discuss that now?" Then a businesslike air animated him. "Ivan," he said to Rainsford, "will supply you with hunting clothes, food, a knife. I suggest you wear moccasins, they leave a poorer trail. I suggest, too, that you avoid the big swamp in the southeast corner of the island. We call it Death Swamp. There's quicksand there. One foolish fellow tried it. The deplorable part of it was that Lazarus followed him. I loved Lazarus, he was the finest hound in my pack.

"Well, I must beg you to excuse me now. I always take a siesta after lunch. You'll hardly have time for a nap, I fear. You'll want to start, no doubt. I shall not follow till dusk. Hunting at night is so much more exciting than by day, don't you think? Au revoir, Mr. Rainsford, au revoir."

General Zaroff, with a deep, courtly bow, strolled from the room. From another door came Ivan. Under one arm he carried khaki hunting clothes, a haversack of food, a leather sheath containing a long-bladed hunting knife; his right hand rested on a cocked revolver thrust in the crimson sash about his waist.

Rainsford had fought his way through the bush for two hours. "I must keep my nerve. I must keep my nerve," he said, through tight teeth.

He had not been entirely clearheaded when the château gates snapped shut behind him. His whole idea at first was to put distance between himself and General Zaroff, and to this end he had plunged along, spurred on by panic. Now he had got a grip on himself, had stopped, and was taking stock of himself and the situation.

He saw that straight flight was futile; inevitably it would bring him face to face with the sea. "I'll give him a trail to follow," muttered Rainsford, and he struck off from the rude path he had been following into the trackless wilderness.

He executed a series of intricate loops, he doubled on his trail again and again, recalling all the lore of the fox hunt, and all the dodges of the fox. Night found him leg-weary, with hands and face lashed by the branches, on a thickly wooded ridge. A big tree with a thick trunk and outspread branches was nearby, and taking care to leave not the slightest mark, he climbed up into the crotch, and stretching out on one of the broad limbs, after a fashion, rested. Rest brought him new confidence and almost a feeling of security. Even so zealous a hunter as General Zaroff could not trace him there, he told himself; only the devil himself could follow that complicated trail through the jungle after dark.

Towards morning, when a dingy gray was varnishing the sky, the cry of some startled bird focused Rainsford's attention. Something was coming by the same winding way Rainsford had come. He flattened himself down on the limb, and through a screen of leaves almost as thick as tapestry he watched. The thing that was approaching was a man.

It was General Zaroff. He made his way along with his eyes fixed in utmost concentration on the ground before him. He paused, almost beneath the tree, dropped to his knees and studied the ground. Rainsford's impulse was to hurl himself down like a panther, but he saw that the general's right hand held something metallic—a small automatic pistol.

The hunter shook his head several times, as if he were puzzled. Then he straightened up and took from his case one of his black cigarettes; its pungent smoke floated up to Rainsford's nostrils.

Rainsford held his breath. The general's eyes had left the ground and were traveling inch by inch up the tree. Rainsford froze there, every muscle tensed for a spring. But the sharp eyes of the hunter stopped before they reached the limb where Rainsford lay; a smile spread over his face. Very deliberately he blew a smoke ring into the air, then he turned his back on the tree and walked carelessly away, back along the trail he had come. The *swish* of the underbrush against his hunting boots grew fainter and fainter.

The pent-up air burst hotly from Rainsford's lungs. His first thought made him sick and numb. The general could follow a trail through the woods at night, he could follow an extremely difficult trail; only by the merest chance had the Cossack failed to see his quarry.

Rainsford's second thought was even more terrible. Why had the general smiled? Why had he turned back? Rainsford did not want to believe what his reason told him was true. The general was playing with him! The general was saving him for another day's sport! The Cossack was the cat; he was the mouse. Then it was that Rainsford knew the full meaning of terror.

"I will not lose my nerve. I will not."

He slid down from the tree and struck off again into the woods. His face was set and he forced the machinery of his mind to function. Three hundred yards from his hiding place he stopped where a huge dead tree leaned precariously on a smaller, living one. Throwing off his sack of food, Rainsford took his knife from its sheath and began to work with all his energy.

The job was finished at last and he threw himself down behind a fallen log a hundred feet away. He did not have long to wait. The cat was coming again to play with the mouse.

Following the trail with the sureness of a bloodhound came General Zaroff. Nothing escaped those searching black eyes, no crushed blade of grass, no bent twig, no mark, no matter how faint, in the moss. So intent was the Cossack on his stalking that he was upon the thing Rainsford had made before he saw it. His foot touched the protruding bough that was the trigger. Even as he touched it, the general sensed his danger and leaped back with the agility of an ape. But he was not quite quick enough; the dead tree struck the general a glancing blow on the shoulder as it fell; he staggered but did not fall; nor did he drop his revolver. He stood there, rubbing his injured shoulder, and Rainsford, with fear again gripping his heart, heard the general's mocking laugh ring through the jungle.

"Rainsford," called the general, "if you are within sound of my voice, as I suppose you are, let me congratulate you. Not many men know how to make a Malay man-catcher. Luckily for me, I too have hunted in Malacca. You are proving of interest, Mr. Rainsford. I am going now to have my wound dressed; it's only a slight one. But I shall be back. I shall be back."

When the general, nursing his bruised shoulder, had gone, Rainsford took up flight again. It was flight now, a desperate, hopeless flight. Dusk came, then darkness, and still he pressed on. The ground grew softer under his moccasins, the vegetation grew ranker, denser, insects bit him savagely. Then, as he stepped forwards, his foot sank into the ooze. He tried to wrench it back, but the muck sucked viciously at his foot. With a violent effort he tore his foot loose. He knew where he was now. Death Swamp and its quicksand. The softness of the earth gave him an idea. He stepped back from the quicksand a dozen feet or so and began to dig. The pit grew deeper; when it was above his shoulders he climbed out and from some hard saplings cut stakes

and sharpened them to a fine point. These stakes he planted in
the bottom of the pit with the points sticking up. With flying
fingers he wove a rough carpet of weeds and branches and with it
he covered the mouth of the pit. Then, wet with sweat and
aching with tiredness, he crouched behind the stump of a
lightning-charred tree.

He knew his pursuer was coming; he heard the padding sound
of feet on the soft earth, and the night breeze brought him the
perfume of the general's cigarette. Rainsford, crouching there,
lived a year in a minute. Then he felt an impulse to cry aloud
with joy, for he heard the sharp crackle of the breaking branches
as the cover of the pit gave way; he heard the sharp scream of pain
as the pointed stakes found their mark. He leaped up from his
place of concealment. Then he cowered back. Three feet from the
pit a man was standing with an electric torch in his hand.

"You've done well, Rainsford," the voice of the general called.
"Your Burmese tiger pit has claimed one of my best dogs. Again
you score. I think, Mr. Rainsford, I'll see what you can do
against a whole pack. I'm going home for a rest now. Thank you
for a most amusing evening."

At daybreak Rainsford, lying near the swamp, was awakened
by a sound that made him know that he had new things to learn
about fear. It was the baying of a pack of hounds. For a moment
he stood there, thinking. An idea that held a wild chance came to
him, and tightening his belt, he headed away from the swamp.

The baying of the hounds drew nearer, then still nearer,
nearer, ever nearer. On a ridge Rainsford climbed a tree. Down a
watercourse, not a quarter of a mile away, he could see the bush
moving. Straining his eyes, he saw the lean figure of General
Zaroff; just ahead of him, Rainsford made out another figure
whose wide shoulders surged through the tall jungle weeds; it
was the giant Ivan, holding the pack in leash.

They would be on him any minute now. His mind worked

frantically. He thought of a native trick he had learned in Uganda. He slid down the tree. He caught hold of a springy young sapling and to it he fastened his hunting knife, with the blade pointing down the trail; with a bit of wild grapevine he tied back the sapling. Then he ran for his life. The hounds raised their voices as they hit the fresh scent.

He had to stop to get his breath. The baying of the hounds stopped abruptly and Rainsford's heart stopped, too. They must have reached the knife.

He shinned excitedly up a tree and looked back, but the hope in his brain died, for he saw in the shallow valley that General Zaroff was still on his feet. Ivan was not. The knife driven by the recoil of the springing tree had not wholly failed.

Rainsford had hardly tumbled to the ground when the pack took up the cry again.

"Nerve, nerve, nerve!" he panted, as he dashed along. A blue gap showed between the trees dead ahead. Rainsford forced himself on towards that gap. It was the shore of the sea. Across a cove he could see the gloomy gray stone of the château. Twenty feet below him the sea rumbled and hissed. Rainsford hesitated. He heard the hounds. Then he leaped far out into the sea. . . .

When the general and his pack reached the place by the sea, the Cossack stopped. For some minutes he stood regarding the blue green expanse of water. He shrugged his shoulders. Then he sat down, took a drink of brandy from a silver flask, and hummed a bit from *Madame Butterfly*.

General Zaroff had an exceedingly good dinner in his great panelled dining hall that evening. Two slight annoyances kept him from perfect enjoyment. One was the thought that it would be difficult to replace Ivan, the other was that his quarry had escaped him. In his library he read, to soothe himself, from the works of Marcus Aurelius. At ten he went up to his bedroom. He was deliciously tired, he said to himself, as he locked himself in. There was a little moonlight, so before turning on his light he went to the window and looked down at the courtyard. He could see the great hounds and called, "Better luck another time," to them. Then he switched on the light.

A man who had been hiding in the curtains of the bed was standing there.

"Rainsford!" cried the general. "How in God's name did you get here?"

"Swam," said Rainsford. "I found it quicker than walking through the jungle."

The general sucked in his breath and smiled. "I congratulate you," he said. "You have won the game."

Rainsford did not smile. "I am still a beast at bay," he said, in a low, hoarse voice. "Get ready, General Zaroff."

The general made one of his deepest bows. "I see," he said. "Splendid! One of us is to furnish a repast for the hounds. The other will sleep in this very excellent bed. On guard, Rainsford. . . ."

He had never slept in a better bed, Rainsford decided.

Return to the Sabbath

ROBERT BLOCH

IT'S NOT THE KIND OF STORY that the columnists like to print; it's not the yarn press agents love to tell. When I was still in the public relations department at the studio, they wouldn't let me break it. I knew better than to try, for no paper would print such a tale.

We publicity men must present Hollywood as a gay place; a world of glamor and stardust. We capture only the light, but underneath the light there must always be shadows. I've always known that—it's been my job to gloss over those shadows for years—but the events of which I speak form a disturbing pattern too strange to be withheld. The shadow of these incidents is not *human*.

It's been the cursed weight of the whole affair that has proved my own mental undoing. That's why I resigned from the studio post, I guess. I wanted to forget, if I could. And now I know that the only way to relieve my mind is to tell the story. I must break the yarn, come what may. Then perhaps I can forget Karl Jorla's eyes. . . .

1

The affair dates back to one September evening almost three years ago. Les Kincaid and I were slumming down on Main Street in Los Angeles that night. Les is an assistant producer up at the studio, and there was some purpose in his visit; he was looking for authentic types to fill minor roles in a gangster film he was doing. Les was peculiar that way; he preferred the real article, rather than the casting bureau's ready-made imitations.

We'd been wandering around for some time, as I recall, past the great stone Chows that guard the narrow alleys of Chinatown, over through the tourist trap that is Olivera Street, and back along the flophouses of lower Main. We walked by the cheap burlesque houses, jostling our way through the usual Saturday night slumming parties.

We were both rather weary of it all. That's why, I suppose, the dingy little theatre appealed to us.

"Let's go in and sit down for a while," Les suggested. "I'm tired."

Even a Main Street burlesque show has seats in it, and I felt ready for a nap. The callipygy of the stage attraction did not appeal to me, but I acceded to the suggestion and purchased our tickets.

We entered, sat down, suffered through two striptease dances, an incredibly ancient blackout sketch, and a "Grand Finale." Then, as is the custom in such places, the stage darkened and the screen flickered into life.

We got ready for our doze, then. The pictures shown in these houses are usually ancient specimens of the "quickie" variety; fillers provided to clear the house. As the first blaring notes of the sound track heralded the title of the opus, I closed my eyes, slouched lower in my seat, and mentally beckoned to Morpheus.

I was jerked back to reality by a sharp dig in the ribs. Les was nudging me and whispering.

"Look at this," he murmured, prodding my reluctant body into wakefulness. "Ever see anything like it?"

I glanced up at the screen. What I expected to find I do not know, but I saw—*horror*.

There was a country graveyard, shadowed by ancient trees through which flickered rays of mildewed moonlight. It was an old graveyard, with rotting headstones set in grotesque angles as they leered up at the midnight sky.

The camera cut down on one grave, a fresh one. The music on the sound track grew louder, in cursed climax. But I forgot camera and film as I watched. That grave was reality—hideous reality.

The grave was *moving!*

The earth beside the headstone was heaving and churning, as though it were being dug out. Not from above, but from *below*. It quaked upward ever so slowly; terribly. Little clods fell. The sod pulsed out in a steady stream and little rills of earth kept falling in the moonlight as though there were something clawing the dirt away . . . something clawing from beneath.

That something—it would soon appear. And I began to be afraid. I—I didn't want to see what it was. The clawing from below was not natural; it held a purpose *not* altogether *human*.

Yet I had to look. I had to see *him*—it—emerge. The sod cascaded in a mound, and then I was staring at the edge of the grave, looking down at the black hole that gaped like a corpse's mouth in the moonlight. Something was coming out.

Something slithered through that fissure, fumbled at the side of the opening. It clutched the ground above the grave, and in the baleful beams of that demon moon I knew it to be a human hand. A thin, white human hand that held but half its flesh. The hand of a lich, a skeleton claw. . . .

A second talon gripped the other side of the excavation top.

[35]

And now, slowly, insidiously, arms emerged. Naked, fleshless arms.

They crawled across the earth sides like leprous white serpents. The arms of a cadaver, a rising cadaver. It was pulling itself up. And as it emerged, a cloud fell across the moonpath. The light faded to shadows as the bulky head and shoulders came into view. One could see nothing, and I was thankful.

But the cloud was falling away from the moon now. In a second the face would be revealed. The face of the thing from the grave, the resurrected visage of that which should be rotted in death—what would it be?

The shadows fell back. A figure rose out of the grave, and the face turned toward me. I looked and saw—

Well, you've been to "horror pictures." You know what one usually sees. The "ape-man," or the "maniac," or the "death's head." The papier-mâché grotesquerie of the makeup artist. The "skull" of the dead.

I saw none of that. Instead, there was *horror*. It was the face of a child, I thought, at first; no, not a child, but a man with a child's soul. The face of a poet, perhaps, unwrinkled and calm. Long hair framed a high forehead; crescent eyebrows tilted over closed lids. The nose and mouth were thin and finely chiseled. Over the entire countenance was written an unearthly peace. It was as though the man were in a sleep of somnambulism or catalepsy. And then the face grew larger, the moonlight brighter, and I saw—more.

The sharper light disclosed tiny touches of evil. The thin lips were fretted, maggot-kissed. The nose had *crumbled* at the nostrils. The forehead was flaked with putrefaction, and the dark hair was dead, encrusted with slime. There were shadows in the bony ridges beneath the closed eyes. Even now, the skeletal arms were up, and bony fingers brushed at those dead pits as the rotted lids fluttered apart. The eyes opened.

They were wide, staring, flaming—and in them was the grave. They were eyes that had closed in death and opened in the coffin under earth. They were eyes that had seen the body rot and the soul depart to mingle in worm-ravened darkness below. They were eyes that held an alien life, a life so dreadful as to animate the cadaver's body and force it to claw its way back to outer earth. They were *hungry* eyes—triumphant, now, as they gazed in graveyard moonlight on a world they had never known before. They hungered for the world as only Death can hunger for Life. And they blazed out of the corpse-pallid face in icy joy.

Then the cadaver began to walk. It lurched between the graves, lumbered before ancient tombs. It shambled through the forest night until it reached a road. Then it turned up that road slowly . . . slowly.

And the hunger in those eyes flamed again as the lights of a city flared below. Death was preparing to mingle with men.

2

I sat through all this entranced. Only a few minutes had elapsed, but I felt as though uncounted ages had passed unheeded. The film went on. Les and I didn't exchange a word, but we watched.

The plot was rather routine after that. The dead man was a scientist whose wife had been stolen from him by a young doctor. The doctor had tended him in his last illness and unwittingly administered a powerful narcotic with cataleptic effects.

The dialog was foreign, and I could not place it. All of the actors were unfamiliar to me, and the setting and photography were quite unusual—unorthodox treatment as in *The Cabinet of Dr. Caligari* and other psychological films.

There was one scene where the living-dead man became enthroned as archpriest at a Black Mass ceremonial, and there was a little child. . . . His eyes as he plunged the knife . . .

He kept—*decaying* throughout the film . . . the Black Mass worshippers knew him as an emissary of Satan, and they kidnapped the wife as sacrifice for his own resurrection . . . the scene with the hysterical woman when she saw and recognized her husband for the first time, and the deep, evil whispering voice in which he revealed his secret to her . . . the final pursuit of the devil-worshippers to the great altar stone in the mountains . . . the death of the resurrected one.

Almost a skeleton in fact now, riddled by bullets and shot from the weapons of the doctor and his neighbors, the dead one crumbled and fell from his seat on the altar stone. And as those eyes glazed in second death, the deep voice boomed out in a prayer to Sathanas. The lich crawled across the ground to the ritual fire, drew painfully erect, and tottered into the flames. And as it stood weaving for a moment in the blaze the lips moved again in infernal prayer, and the eyes implored not the skies, but the earth. The ground opened in a final flash of fire, and the charred corpse fell through. The Master claimed his own. . . .

It was grotesque, almost a fairy tale in its triteness. When the film had flickered off and the orchestra blared the opening for the next "flesh-show" we rose in our seats, conscious once more of our surroundings. The rest of the mongrel audience seemed to be in a stupor almost equal to our own. Wide-eyed Japanese sat staring in the darkness; Filipinos muttered covertly to one another; even the drunken laborers seemed incapable of greeting the "Grand Opening" with their usual ribald hoots.

Trite and grotesque the plot of the film may have been, but the actor who played the lead had instilled it with ghastly reality. He *had* been dead; his eyes *knew*. And the voice was the voice of Lazarus awakened.

Les and I had no need to exchange words. We both felt it. I followed him silently as he went up the stairs to the manager's office.

Edward Relch was glowering over the desk. He showed no pleasure at seeing us barge in. When Les asked him where he had procured the film for this evening and what its name was, he opened his mouth and emitted a cascade of curses.

We learned *Return to the Sabbath* had been sent over by a cheap agency from out Inglewood way, that a Western had been expected, and the "damned foreign junk" substituted by mistake. A hell of a picture this was, for a girl-show! Gave the audience the lousy creeps, and it wasn't even in English! Stinking imported films!

It was some time before we managed to extract the name of the agency from the manager's profane lips. But five minutes after that, Les Kincaid was on the phone speaking to the head of the agency; an hour later we were out at the office. The next morning, Kincaid went to see the big boss, and the following day I was told to announce for publication that Karl Jorla, the Austrian horror-star, had been signed by cable to our studio; and he was leaving at once for the United States.

I printed these items, gave all the buildup I could. But after the initial announcements I was stopped dead. Everything had happened too swiftly; we knew nothing about this man Jorla, really. Subsequent cables to Austrian and German studios failed to disclose any information about the fellow's private life. He had evidently never played in any film prior to *Return to the Sabbath*. He was utterly unknown. The film had never been shown widely abroad, and it was only by mistake that the Inglewood agency had obtained a copy and run it here in the United States. Audience reaction could not be learned, and the film was not scheduled for general release unless English titles could be dubbed in.

I was up a stump. Here we had the "find" of the year, and I couldn't get enough material out to make it known!

We expected Karl Jorla to arrive in two weeks, however. I was told to get to work on him as soon as he got in, then flood the news agencies with stories. Three of our best writers were working on a special production for him already; the Big Boss meant to handle it himself. It would be similar to the foreign film, for that "return from the dead" sequence must be included.

Jorla arrived on October seventh. He put up at a hotel; the studio sent down its usual welcoming committee, took him out to the lot for formal testing, then turned him over to me.

I met the man for the first time in the little dressing room they had assigned him. I'll never forget that afternoon of our first meeting, or my first sight of him as I entered the door.

What I expected to see I don't know. But what I did see amazed me. For Karl Jorla was the dead-alive man of the screen *in life.*

The features were not fretted, of course. But he was tall, and almost as cadaverously thin as in his role; his face was pallid, and his eyes blue-circled. And the eyes were the dead eyes of the movie; the deep, *knowing* eyes!

The booming voice greeted me in hesitant English. Jorla smiled with his lips at my obvious discomfiture, but the expression of the eyes never varied in their alien strangeness.

Somewhat hesitantly I explained my office and my errand. "No pub-leecity," Jorla intoned. "I do not weesh to make known what is affairs of mine own doeeng."

I gave him the usual arguments. How much he understood I cannot say, but he was adamant. I learned only a little; that he had been born in Prague, lived in wealth until the upheavals of the European depression, and entered film work only to please a director friend of his. This director had made the picture in which Jorla played, for private showings only. By mischance a print had been released and copied for general circulation. It had all been a mistake. However, the American film offer had come opportunely, since Jorla wanted to leave Austria at once.

"After the feelm ap-pear, I am in bad lights weeth my— friends," he explained slowly. "They do not weesh it to be shown, that cere-monee."

"The Black Mass?" I asked. "Your *friends?*"

"Yes. The wor-ship of Lucifer. It was real, you know."

Was he joking? No—I couldn't doubt the man's sincerity. There was no room for mirth in those alien eyes. And then I knew what he meant, what he so casually revealed. He had been a devil-worshipper himself—he and that director. They had made the film and meant it for private display in their own occult circles. No wonder he sought escape abroad!

It was incredible, save that I knew Europe, and the dark Northern mind. The worship of Evil continues today in Budapest, Prague, Berlin. And he, Karl Jorla, the horror-actor, admitted to being one of them!

"What a story!" I thought. And then I realized that it could, of course, never be printed! A horror-star admitting *belief* in the parts he played? Absurd!

All the features about Boris Karloff played up the fact that he was a gentle man who found true peace in raising a garden. Lugosi was pictured as a sensitive neurotic, tortured by the roles he played in the films. Atwill was a socialite and a stage star. And Peter Lorre was always written up as being gentle as a lamb, a quiet student whose ambition was to play comedy parts.

No, it would never do to break the story of Jorla's devil-worship. And he was so damnably reticent about his private affairs!

I sought out Kincaid after the termination of our unsatisfactory interview. I told him what I had encountered and asked for advice. He gave it.

"The old line," he counseled. "Mystery man. We say nothing about him until the picture is released. After that I have a hunch things will work out for themselves. The fellow is a marvel. So don't bother about stories until the film is canned."

Consequently I abandoned publicity efforts in Karl Jorla's direction. Now I am very glad I did so, for there is no one to remember his name, or suspect the horror that was soon to follow.

4

The script was finished. The front office approved. Stage Four was under construction; the casting director got busy. Jorla was at the studio every day; Kincaid himself was teaching him English. The part was one in which very few words were needed, and Jorla proved a brilliant pupil, according to Les.

But Les was not as pleased as he should have been about it all. He came to me one day about a week before production and unburdened himself. He strove to speak lightly about the affair, but I could tell that he felt worried.

The gist of his story was very simple. Jorla was behaving strangely. He had had trouble with the front office; he refused to give the studio his living address, and it was known that he had checked out of his hotel several days after first arriving in Hollywood.

Nor was that all. He wouldn't talk about his part, or volunteer any information about interpretation. He seemed to be quite uninterested—admitting frankly to Kincaid that his only reason for signing a contract was to leave Europe.

He told Kincaid what he had told me—about the devil-worshippers. And he hinted at more. He spoke of being followed, muttered about "avengers" and "hunters who waited." He seemed to feel that the witch-cult was angry at him for the violation of secrets, and held him responsible for the release of *Return to the Sabbath*. That, he explained, was why he would not give his address, nor speak of his past life for publication. That is why he must use very heavy makeup in his film debut here. He felt at times as though he were being watched, or followed. There were many foreigners here . . . too many.

"What the devil can I do with a man like that?" Kincaid exploded, after he had explained this to me. "He's insane, or a fool. And I confess that he's too much like his screen character to please me. The damned casual way in which he professes to have dabbled in devil-worship and sorcery! He believes all this, and—well, I'll tell you the truth, I came here today because of the last thing he spoke of to me this morning.

"He came down to the office, and at first when he walked in I didn't know him. The dark glasses and muffler helped, of course, but he himself had changed. He was trembling, and walked with a stoop. And when he spoke his voice was like a groan. He showed me—this."

Kincaid handed me the clipping. It was from the London *Times*, through European press dispatches. A short paragraph, giving an account of Fritz Ohmmen, the Austrian film director. He had been found strangled in a Paris garret, and his body had been frightfully mutilated; it mentioned an inverted cross branded on his stomach above the ripped entrails. Police were seeking the murderer.

I handed the clipping back in silence. "So what?" I asked. But I had already guessed his answer.

"Fritz Ohmmen," Kincaid said slowly, "was the director of the picture in which Karl Jorla played; the director who, with Jorla, knew the devil-worshippers. Jorla says that he fled to Paris, and that *they* sought him out."

I was silent.

"Mess," grunted Kincaid. "I've offered Jorla police protection, and he's refused. I can't coerce him under the terms of our contract. As long as he plays the part, he's secure with us. But he has the jitters. And I'm getting them."

He stormed out. I couldn't help him. I sat thinking of Karl Jorla, who believed in devil-gods; worshipped, and betrayed them. And I could have smiled at the absurdity of it all if I hadn't seen the man on the screen and watched his evil eyes. He *knew!* It was then that I began to feel thankful we had not given Jorla any publicity. I had a hunch.

During the next few days I saw Jorla but seldom. The rumors, however, began to trickle in. There had been an influx of foreign "sightseers" at the studio gates. Someone had attempted to crash through the barriers in a racing car. An extra in a mob scene over on Lot Six had been found carrying an automatic beneath his vest; when apprehended he had been lurking under the executive office windows. They had taken him down to headquarters, and so far the man had refused to talk. He was a German. . . .

Jorla came to the studio every day in a shuttered car. He was bundled up to the eyes. He trembled constantly. His English lessons went badly. He spoke to no one. He hired two men to ride with him in his car. They were armed.

A few days later news came that the German extra talked. He was evidently a pathological case . . . he babbled wildly of a "Black Cult of Lucifer" known to some of the foreigners around town. It was a secret society purporting to worship the Devil, with vague connections in the mother countries. He had been "chosen" to avenge a wrong. More than that he dared not say, but he did give an address where the police might find cult headquarters. The place, a dingy house in Glendale, was quite deserted, of course. It was a queer old house with a secret cellar beneath the basement, but everything seemed to have been abandoned. The man was being held for examination by an alienist.

I heard this report with deep misgivings. I knew something of Los Angeles' and Hollywood's heterogeneous foreign population; God knows, Southern California has attracted mystics and occultists from all over the world. I've even heard rumors about stars being mixed up in unsavory secret societies, things one would never dare to admit in print. And Jorla was afraid.

That afternoon I tried to trail his black car as it left the studio for his mysterious home, but I lost track in the winding reaches of Topanga Canyon. It had disappeared into the secret twilight of the purple hills, and I knew then that there was nothing I could do. Jorla had his own defenses, and if they failed, we at the studio could not help.

That was the evening he disappeared. At least he did not show up the next morning at the studio, and production was to start in two days. We heard about it. The boss and Kincaid were frantic. The police were called in, and I did my best to hush things up. When Jorla did not appear the following morning I went to Kincaid and told him about my following the car to Topanga Canyon. The police went to work. Next morning was production.

We spent a sleepless night of fruitless vigil. There was no word. Morning came, and there was unspoken dread in Kincaid's eyes as he faced me across the office table. Eight o'clock. We got up and walked silently across the lot to the studio cafeteria. Black coffee was badly needed; we hadn't had a police report for hours. We passed Stage Four, where the Jorla crew was at work. The noise of hammers was mockery. Jorla, we felt, would never face a camera today, if ever.

Bleskind, the director of the untitled horror opus, came out of the stage office as we passed.

His paunchy body quivered as he grasped Kincaid's lapels and piped, "Any news?"

Kincaid shook his head slowly. Bleskind thrust a cigar into his tense mouth.

"We're shooting ahead," he snapped. "We'll shoot around Jorla. If he doesn't show up when we finish the scenes in which he won't appear, we'll get another actor. But we can't wait." The squat director bustled back to the stage.

Moved by a sudden impulse, Kincaid grasped my arm and propelled me after Bleskind's waddling form.

"Let's see the opening shots," he suggested. "I want to see what kind of a story they've given him."

We entered Stage Four.

A Gothic castle, the ancestral home of Baron Ulmo. A dark, gloomy stone crypt of spidery horror. Cobwebbed, dust-shrouded, deserted by men and given over to the rats by day and the unearthly horrors that crept by night. An altar stood by the crypt, an altar of evil, the great black stone on which the ancient Baron Ulmo and his devil-cult had held their sacrifices. Now, in the pit beneath the altar, the baron lay buried. Such was the legend.

According to the first shot scheduled, Sylvia Channing, the heroine, was exploring the castle. She had inherited the place and taken it over with her young husband. In this scene she was to see the altar for the first time, read the inscription on its base. The inscription was to prove an unwitting invocation, opening up the crypt beneath the altar and awakening Jorla, as Baron Ulmo, from the dead. He was to rise from the crypt then, and walk. It was at this point that the scene would terminate, due to Jorla's strange absence.

The setting was magnificently handled. Kincaid and I took our places beside Director Bleskind as the shot opened. Sylvia Channing walked out on the set; the signals were given, lights flashed, and the action began.

It was pantomimic. Sylvia walked across the cobwebbed floor, noticed the altar, examined it. She stooped to read the inscription, then whispered it aloud. There was a drone, as the opening of the altar-crypt was mechanically begun. The altar swung aside and the black gaping pit was revealed. The upper cameras swung to Sylvia's face. She was to stare at the crypt in horror, and she did it most magnificently. In the picture she would be watching Jorla emerge.

Bleskind prepared to give the signal to cut action. Then— *Something emerged from the crypt!*

It was dead, that thing—that horror with a mask of faceless flesh. Its lean body was clothed in rotting rags, and on its chest was a bloody crucifix, inverted—carved out of dead flesh. The eyes blazed loathsomely. It was Baron Ulmo, rising from the dead. *And it was Karl Jorla!*

The makeup was perfect. His eyes were dead, just as in the other film. The lips seemed shredded again, the mouth even more ghastly in its slitted blackness. And the touch of the bloody crucifix was immense.

Bleskind nearly swallowed his cigar when Jorla appeared. Quickly he controlled himself, silently signalled the men to proceed with the shooting. We strained forward, watching every move, but Les Kincaid's eyes held a wonder akin to my own.

Jorla was acting as never before. He moved slowly, as a corpse must move. As he raised himself from the crypt, each tiny effort seemed to cause him utter agony. The scene was soundless; Sylvia had fainted. But Jorla's lips moved, and we heard a faint whispering murmur which heightened the horror. Now the grisly cadaver was almost half out of the crypt. It strained upward, still murmuring. The bloody crucifix of flesh gleamed redly on the chest. . . . I thought of the one found on the body of the murdered foreign director, Fritz Ohmmen, and realized where Jorla had gotten the idea.

The corpse strained up . . . it was to rise now . . . up . . . and then, with a sudden rictus, the body stiffened and slid back into the crypt.

Who screamed first I do not know. But the screaming continued after the prop boys had rushed to the crypt and looked down at what lay within.

When I reached the brink of the pit I screamed, too.

For it was utterly empty.

5

I wish there were nothing more to tell. The papers never knew. The police hushed things up. The studio is silent, and the production was dropped immediately. But matters did not stop there. There was a sequel to that horror on Stage Four.

Kincaid and I cornered Bleskind. There was no need of any explanation; how could what we had just seen be explained in any sane way?

Jorla had disappeared; no one had let him into the studio; no makeup man had given him his attention. Nobody had seen him enter the crypt. He had appeared in the scene, then disappeared. The crypt was empty.

These were the facts. Kincaid told Bleskind what to do. The film was developed immediately, though two of the technicians fainted. We three sat in the projection booth and watched the morning's rushes flicker across the screen. The sound track was specially dubbed in.

That scene—Sylvia walking and reading the incantation—the pit opening—and God, when *nothing* emerged!

Nothing but that great red scar suspended in midair—that great inverted crucifix cut in bleeding flesh; no Jorla visible at all! That bleeding cross in the air, and then the mumbling . . .

Jorla—the thing—whatever it was—had mumbled a few syllables on emerging from the crypt. The sound track had picked them up. And we couldn't see anything but that scar; yet we heard Jorla's voice now coming from nothingness. We heard what he kept repeating, as he fell back into the crypt.

It was an address in Topanga Canyon.

The lights flickered on, and it was good to see them. Kincaid phoned the police and directed them to the address given on the sound track.

We waited, the three of us, in Kincaid's office, waited for the police call. We drank, but did not speak. Each of us was thinking of Karl Jorla the devil-worshipper who had betrayed his faith; of his fear of vengeance. We thought of the director's death, and the bloody crucifix on his chest; remembered Jorla's disappearance. And then that ghastly ghost-thing on the screen, the bloody thing that hung in midair as Jorla's voice groaned the address . . .

The phone rang.

I picked it up. It was the police department. They gave their report. I fainted.

It was several minutes before I came to. It was several more minutes before I opened my mouth and spoke.

"They've found Karl Jorla's body at the address given on the screen," I whispered. "He was lying dead in an old shack up in the hills. He had been—murdered. There was a bloody cross, inverted on his chest. They think it was the work of some fanatics, because the place was filled with books on sorcery and black magic. They say—"

I paused. Kincaid's eyes commanded. "Go on."

"They say," I murmured, "that Jorla had been dead for at least three days."

The Amorous Ghost

ENID BAGNOLD

IT WAS FIVE O'CLOCK on a summer morning. The birds, who
had woken at three, had long scattered about their duties. The
white, plain house, blinkered and green-shuttered, stood four-
square to its soaking lawns, and up and down on the grass, his
snow boots planting dark blots on the gray dew, walked the
owner. His hair was uncombed, he wore his pyjamas and an
overcoat, and at every turn at the end of the lawn he looked up at
a certain window, that of his own and his wife's bedroom, where,
as on every other window on the long front, the green shutters
lay neatly back against the wall and the cream curtains hung
down in heavy folds.

The owner of the house, strangely and uncomfortably on his
lawns instead of in his bed, rubbed his chilly hands and
continued his tramp. He had no watch on his wrist, but when the
stable clock struck six he entered the house, and passing through
the still hall he went up to his bathroom. The water was
lukewarm in the taps from the night before, and he took a bath.
As he left the bathroom for his dressing-room he heard the

stirring of the first housemaid in the living-rooms below, and at seven o'clock he rang for his butler to lay out his clothes.

As the same thing had happened the day before, the butler was half prepared for the bell; yawning and incensed but ready dressed.

"Good morning," said Mr. Templeton rather suddenly. It was a greeting which he never gave, but he wished to try the quality of his voice. Finding it steady he went on, and gave an order for a melon from the greenhouse.

For breakfast he had very little appetite, and when he had finished the melon he unfolded the newspaper. The door of the dining-room opened, and the parlormaid and housemaid came in and gave him their notice.

"A month from today, sir," repeated the parlormaid to bridge the silence that followed.

"It's nothing to do with me," he said in a low voice. "Your mistress is coming home tonight. You must tell her of these things."

They left the room.

"What's the matter with those girls?" said Mr. Templeton to the butler who came in.

"They haven't spoken to me, sir," said the butler untruly, "but I gather there has been an upset."

"Because I chose to get up early on a summer morning?" asked Mr. Templeton with an effort.

"Yes, sir. And there were other reasons."

"Which were?"

"The housemaid," said the butler with detachment, as though he were speaking of the movements of a fly, "has found your bedroom, sir, strewn with clothes."

"With *my* clothes?" said Mr. Templeton.

"No, sir."

Mr. Templeton sat down. "A nightgown?" he said weakly, as though appealing for human understanding.

"Yes, sir."

"More than one?"

"Two, sir."

"Good God!" said Mr. Templeton, and walked to the window whistling shakily.

The butler cleared the table quietly and left the room.

"There's no question about it," said Mr. Templeton under his breath. "She was undressing . . . behind the chair."

After breakfast he walked down his two fields and through a wood with the idea of talking to Mr. George Casson. But George had gone to London for the day, and Mr. Templeton, faced with the polish on the front door, the polish on the parlormaid, and the sober look of the *Morning Post* folded on the hall table, felt that it was just as well that he had not after all to confide his incredible story. He walked back again, steadied by the air and exercise.

"I'll telephone to Hettie," he decided, "and make sure that she is coming tonight."

He rang up his wife, told her that he was well, that all was well, and heard with satisfaction that she was coming down that night after her dinner-party, catching the eleven-thirty, arriving at twelve-fifteen at the station.

"There is no train before at all," she said. "I sent around to the station to see, and owing to the strike they run none between seven-fifteen and eleven-thirty."

"Then I'll send the car to the station and you'll be here at half-past twelve. I may be in bed, as I'm tired."

"You're not ill?"

"No. I've had a bad night."

It was not until the afternoon, after a good luncheon and a whisky-and-soda, that Mr. Templeton went up to his bedroom to have a look at it.

The cream curtains hung lightly blowing in the window. By the fireplace stood a high, wing, grandfather chair upholstered in patterned rep. Opposite the chair and the fireplace was the

double bed, in one side of which Mr. Templeton had lain
working at his papers the night before. He walked up to the
chair, put his hands in his pockets, and stood looking down at it.
Then he crossed to the chest of drawers and drew out a drawer.
On the right-hand side were Hettie's vests and chemises, neatly
pressed and folded. On the left was a pile, folded but not pressed,
of Hettie's nightgowns. Mr. Templeton noted the crumples and
creases on the silk.

"Evidence, evidence," he said, walking to the window, "that
something happened in this room after I left it this morning. The
maids believe they found a strange woman's nightgowns crum-
pled on the floor. As a matter of fact they are Hettie's
nightgowns. I suppose a doctor would say I'd done it myself in a
trance.

"Two nights ago?" he thought, looking again at the bed. It
seemed a week. The night before last as he lay working, propped
up on pillows and cushions and his papers spread over the bed, he
had glanced up, absorbed, at two o'clock in the morning and
traced the pattern on the grandfather chair as it stood facing the
empty grate with its back towards him, just as he had left it
when he had got into bed. It was then that he had seen the two
hands hanging idly over the back of the chair as though an unseen
owner were kneeling in the seat. His eyes stared, and a cold fear
wandered down his spine. He sat without moving and watched
the hands.

Ten minutes passed, and the hands were withdrawn quickly as
though the occupant of the chair had silently changed its
position.

Still he watched, propped, stiffening, on his pillows, and as
time went on he fought the impression down. "Tired," he said.
"One's read of it. The brain reflecting something." His heart
quietened, and cautiously he settled himself a little lower and
tried to sleep. He did not dare straighten the litter of papers
around him, but with the light on he lay there till the dawn lit
the yellow paint on the wall. At five he got up, sleepless, his eyes

still on the back of the grandfather chair, and without his dressing-gown or slippers he left the room. In the hall he found an overcoat and his warm snow boots behind a chest, and unbolting the front door he tramped the lawn in the dew.

On the second night (*last* night) he had worked as before. So completely had he convinced himself after a day of fresh air that his previous night's experience had been the result of his own imagination, his eyesight and his mind hallucinated by his work, that he had not even remembered (as he had meant to do) to turn the grandfather chair with its seat towards him. Now, as he worked in bed, he glanced from time to time at its patterned and concealing back, and wished vaguely that he had thought to turn it round.

He had not worked more than two hours before he knew that there was something going on in the chair.

"Who's there?" he called. The slight movement he had heard ceased for a moment, then began again. For a second he thought he saw the tip of a mound of fair hair showing over the top. There was a sound of scuffling in the chair, and some object flew out and landed with a bump on the floor below the field of his vision. Five minutes went by, and after a fresh scuffle a hand shot up and laid a bundle, white and stiff, with what seemed a small arm hanging, on the back of the chair.

Mr. Templeton had had two bad nights and a great many hours of emotion. When he grasped that the object was a corset with a suspender swinging from it, something bumped unevenly in his heart, a million black motes like a cloud of flies swam in his eyeballs; he fainted.

He woke up, and the room was dark, the light off, and he felt a little sick. Turning in bed to find comfort for his body, he remembered that he had been in the middle of a crisis of fear. He looked about him in the dark, and saw again the dawn on the curtains. Then he heard a chink by the washstand, several feet nearer to his bed than the grandfather chair. He was not alone; the thing was still in the room.

By the faint light from the curtains he could just see that his visitor was by the washstand. There was a gentle clinking of china and a sound of water, and dimly he could see a woman standing.

"Undressing," he said to himself, "washing."

His gorge rose at the thought that came to him. Was it possible that the woman was coming to bed?

It was that thought that had driven him with a wild rush from the room, and sent him marching for a second time up and down his gray and dewy lawns.

"And now," thought Mr. Templeton as he stood in the neat bedroom in the afternoon light and looked around him, "Hettie's *got* to believe in the unfaithful or the supernatural."

He crossed to the grandfather chair, and taking it in his two hands was about to push it onto the landing. But he paused. "I'll leave it where it is tonight," he thought, "and go to bed as usual. For both our sakes I must find out something more about all this."

Spending the rest of the afternoon out-of-doors, he played golf after tea, and after eating a very light dinner he went to bed. His head ached badly from lack of sleep, but he was pleased to notice that his heart beat steadily. He took a couple of aspirin tablets to ease his head, and with a light novel settled himself down in bed to read and watch. Hettie would arrive at half-past twelve, and the butler was waiting up to let her in. Sandwiches, nicely covered from the air, were placed ready for her on a tray in a corner of the bedroom.

It was now eleven. He had an hour and a half to wait. "She may come at any time," he said (thinking of his visitor). He had turned the grandfather chair towards him, so that he could see the seat.

A quarter of an hour went by, and his head throbbed so violently that he put the book on his knees and altered the lights, turned out the brilliant reading lamp, and switched on the light which illumined the large face of the clock over the mantelpiece, so that he sat in shadow. Five minutes later he was asleep.

He lay with his face buried in the pillow, the pain still drumming in his head, aware of his headache even at the bottom of his sleep. Dimly he heard his wife arrive, and murmured a hope to himself that she would not wake him. A slight movement rustled around him as she entered the room and undressed, but his pain was so bad that he could not bring himself to give a sign of life, and soon, while he clung to his half-sleep, he felt the bedclothes gently lifted and heard her slip in beside him.

Feeling chilly, he drew his blanket closer around him. It was as though a draft was blowing about him in the bed, dispelling the mists of sleep and bringing him to himself. He felt a touch of remorse at his lack of welcome, and putting out his hand he sought his wife's beneath the sheet. Finding her wrist, his fingers closed around it. She too was cold, strange, icy, and from her stillness and silence she appeared to be asleep.

"A cold drive from the station," he thought, and held her wrist to warm it as he dozed again. "She is positively chilling the bed," he murmured to himself.

He was awakened by a roar beneath the window and the sweep of a light across the wall of the room. With amazement he heard the bolts shoot back across the front door. On the illuminated face of the clock over the fireplace he saw the hands standing at twenty-seven minutes past twelve. Then Mr. Templeton, still gripping the wrist beside him, heard his wife's clear voice in the hall below.

Tarnhelm, or the Death of My Uncle Robert

SIR HUGH SEYMOUR WALPOLE

1

I WAS, I SUPPOSE, at that time, a peculiar child, peculiar a little by nature, but also because I had spent so much of my young life in the company of people very much older than myself.

After the events that I am now going to relate, some quite indelible mark was set on me. I became then, and have always been since, one of those persons, otherwise insignificant, who have decided, without possibility of change, about certain questions.

Some things, doubted by most of the world, are for these people true and beyond argument: This certainty of theirs gives them a kind of stamp, as though they lived so much in their imagination as to have very little assurance as to what is fact and what fiction. This oddness of theirs puts them apart. If now, at the age of fifty, I am a man with very few friends, it is because, if you like, my Uncle Robert died in a strange manner forty years ago, and I was a witness of his death.

I have never until now given any account of the strange proceedings that occurred at Faildyke Hall on the evening of

Christmas Eve in the year 1890. The incidents of that evening are still remembered very clearly by one or two people, and a kind of legend of my Uncle Robert's death has been carried on into the younger generation. But no one still alive was a witness of them as I was, and I feel it is time that I set them down upon paper.

I write them down without comment. I extenuate nothing; I disguise nothing. I am not, I hope, in any way a vindictive man, but my brief meeting with my Uncle Robert and the circumstances of his death gave my life, even at that early age, a twist difficult for me very readily to forgive.

As to the so-called supernatural element in my story, everyone must judge for himself about that. We deride or we accept according to our natures. If we are built of a certain solid practical material, the probability is that no evidence, however definite, however firsthand, will convince us. If dreams are our daily portion, one dream more or less will scarcely shake our sense of reality.

However, to my story.

My father and mother were in India from my eighth to my thirteenth years. I did not see them, except on two occasions when they visited England. I was an only child, loved dearly by both my parents, who, however, loved one another yet more. They were an exceedingly sentimental couple of the old-fashioned kind. My father was in the Indian Civil Service, and wrote poetry. He even had his epic, *Tantalus: A Poem in Four Cantos,* published at his own expense.

This, added to the fact that my mother had been considered an invalid before he married her, made my parents feel that they bore a very close resemblance to the Brownings, and my father even had a pet name for my mother that sounded curiously like the famous and hideous "Ba."

I was a delicate child, was sent to Mr. Ferguson's Private Academy at the tender age of eight, and spent my holidays as the rather unwanted guest of various relations.

"Unwanted" because I was, I imagine, a difficult child to understand. I had an old grandmother who lived at Folkestone, two aunts who shared a little house in Kensington, an aunt, uncle, and a brood of cousins inhabiting Cheltenham, and two uncles who lived in Cumberland. All these relations, except the two uncles, had their proper share of me and for none of them had I any great affection.

Children were not studied in those days as they are now. I was thin, pale, and bespectacled, aching for affection but not knowing at all how to obtain it: outwardly undemonstrative but inwardly emotional and sensitive, playing games, because of my poor sight, very badly, reading a great deal more than was good for me, and telling myself stories all day and part of every night.

All of my relations tired of me, I fancy, in turn, and at last it was decided that my uncles in Cumberland must do their share. These two were my father's brothers, the eldest of a long family of which he was the youngest. My Uncle Robert, I understood, was nearly seventy, my Uncle Constance some five years younger. I remember always thinking that Constance was a funny name for a man.

My Uncle Robert was the owner of Faildyke Hall, a country house between the lake of Wastwater and the little town of Seascale on the seacoast. Uncle Constance had lived with Uncle Robert for many years. It was decided, after some family correspondence, that the Christmas of this year, 1890, should be spent by me at Faildyke Hall.

I was at this time just eleven years old, thin and skinny, with a bulging forehead, large spectacles, and a nervous, shy manner. I always set out, I remember, on any new adventures with mingled emotions of terror and anticipation. Maybe by *this* time the miracle would occur: I should discover a friend or a fortune, should cover myself with glory in some unexpected way—be at last what I always longed to be, a hero.

I was glad that I was not going to any of my other relations for Christmas, and especially not to my cousins at Cheltenham, who teased and persecuted me and were never free of earsplitting noises. What I wanted most in life was to be allowed to read in peace. I understood that at Faildyke there was a glorious library.

My aunt saw me to the train. I had been presented by my uncle with one of the most gory of Harrison Ainsworth's romances, *The Lancashire Witches,* and I had five bars of chocolate creams, so the journey was as blissfully happy as any experience could be to me at that time. I was permitted to read in peace, and I had just then little more to ask of life.

Nevertheless, as the train puffed its way north, this new country began to force itself on my attention. I had never before been in the North of England, and I was not prepared for the sudden sense of space and freshness that I received.

The naked, unsystematic hills, the freshness of the wind on which the birds seemed to be carried with especial glee, the stone walls that ran like gray ribbons about the moors, and, above all, the vast expanse of sky upon whose surface clouds swam, raced, eddied, and extended as I had never anywhere witnessed.

I sat, lost and absorbed, at my carriage window, and when at last, long after dark had fallen, I heard "Seascale" called by the porter, I was still staring in a sort of romantic dream. When I stepped out onto the little narrow platform and was greeted by the salt tang of the sea wind, my first real introduction to the North Country may be said to have been completed. I am writing now in another part of that same Cumberland country, and beyond my window the line of the fell runs strong and bare against the sky, while below it the lake lies, a fragment of silver glass at the feet of Skiddaw.

It may be that my sense of the deep mystery of this country had its origin in this same strange story that I am now relating. But again perhaps not, for I believe that that first evening arrival at Seascale worked some change in me, so that since then none of the world's beauties—from the crimson waters of Kashmir to the rough glories of our own Cornish coast—can rival for me the sharp, peaty winds and strong, resilient turf of the Cumberland hills.

That was a magical drive in the pony-trap to Faildyke that evening. It was bitterly cold, but I did not seem to mind it. Everything was magical to me.

From the first I could see the great slow hump of Black Combe jet against the frothy clouds of the winter night, and I could hear the sea breaking and the soft rustle of the bare twigs in the hedgerows.

I made, too, the friend of my life that night, for it was Bob Armstrong who was driving the trap. He has often told me since (for although he is a slow man of few words, he likes to repeat the things that seem to him worthwhile) that I struck him as "pitifully lost" that evening on the Seascale platform. I looked, I don't doubt, pinched and cold enough. In any case it was a lucky appearance for me, for I won Armstrong's heart there and then, and he, once he gave it; could never bear to take it back again.

He, on his side, seemed to me gigantic that night. He had, I believe, one of the broadest chests in the world: It was a curse to him, he said, because no ready-made shirts would ever fit him.

I sat in close to him because of the cold; he was very warm, and I could feel his heart beating like a steady clock inside his rough coat. It beat for me that night, and it has beaten for me, I'm glad to say, ever since.

In truth, as things turned out, I needed a friend. I was nearly asleep and stiff all over my little body when I was handed down from the trap and at once led into what seemed to me an immense hall crowded with the staring heads of slaughtered animals and smelling of straw.

I was so sadly weary that my uncles, when I met them in a vast billiard-room in which a great fire roared in a stone fireplace like a demon, seemed to me to be double.

In any case, what an odd pair they were! My Uncle Robert was a little man with gray untidy hair and little sharp eyes hooded by two of the bushiest eyebrows known to humanity. He wore (I remember as though it were yesterday) shabby country clothes of a faded green color, and he had on one finger a ring with a thick red stone.

Another thing that I noticed at once when he kissed me (I detested to be kissed by anybody) was a faint scent that he had, connected at once in my mind with the caraway seeds that there are in seedcakes. I noticed, too, that his teeth were discolored and yellow.

My Uncle Constance I liked at once. He was fat, round, friendly, and clean. Rather a dandy was Uncle Constance. He wore a flower in his buttonhole, and his linen was snowy white in contrast with his brother's.

I noticed one thing, though, at that very first meeting, and that was that before he spoke to me and put his fat arm around my shoulder he seemed to look toward his brother as though for permission. You may say that it was unusual for a boy of my age to notice so much, but in fact I noticed everything at that time. Years and laziness, alas! have slackened my observation.

2

I had a horrible dream that night; it woke me screaming, and brought Bob Armstrong in to quiet me.

My room was large, like all the other rooms that I had seen, and empty, with a great expanse of floor and a stone fireplace like the one in the billiard-room. It was, I afterwards found, next to the servants' quarters. Armstrong's room was next to mine, and Mrs. Spender the housekeeper's beyond his.

Armstrong was then, and is yet, a bachelor. He used to tell me that he loved so many women that he never could bring his mind to choose any one of them. And now he has been too long my personal bodyguard and is too lazily used to my ways to change his condition. He is, moreover, seventy years of age.

Well, what I saw in my dream was this. They had lit a fire for me (and it was necessary; the room was of an icy coldness) and I dreamed that I awoke to see the flames rise to a vast vigor before they died away. In the brilliance of that illumination I was conscious that something was moving in the room. I heard the movement for some little while before I saw anything.

I sat up, my heart hammering, and then to my horror discerned, slinking against the farther wall, the evilest-looking yellow mongrel of a dog that you can fancy.

I find it difficult, I have always found it difficult, to describe exactly the horror of that yellow dog. It lay partly in its color, which was vile, partly in its mean and bony body, but for the most part in its evil head—flat, with sharp little eyes, and jagged yellow teeth.

As I looked at it, it bared those teeth at me and then began to creep, with an indescribably loathsome action, in the direction of my bed. I was at first stiffened with terror. Then, as it neared the bed, its little eyes fixed upon me and its teeth bared, I screamed again and again.

The next I knew was that Armstrong was sitting on my bed, his strong arm about my trembling little body. All I could say over and over was, "The Dog! the Dog! the Dog!"

He soothed me as though he had been my mother.

"See, there's no dog there! There's no one but me!"

I continued to tremble, so he got into bed with me, held me close to him, and it was in his comforting arms that I fell asleep.

3

In the morning I woke to a fresh breeze and a shining sun and the chrysanthemums, orange, crimson, and dun, blowing against the gray stone wall beyond the sloping lawns. So I forgot about my dream. I only knew that I loved Bob Armstrong better than anyone else on earth.

Everyone during the next days was very kind to me. I was so deeply excited by this country, so new to me, that at first I could think of nothing else. Bob Armstrong was Cumbrian from the top of his flaxen head to the thick nails under his boots, and, in grunts and monosyllables, as was his way, he gave me the color of the ground.

There was romance everywhere: smugglers stealing in and out of Drigg and Seascale; the ancient cross in Gosforth churchyard; Ravenglass, with all its seabirds, once a port of splendor.

Muncaster Castle and Broughton and black Wastwater with the grim Screes, Black Combe, upon whose broad back the shadows were always dancing—even the little station at Seascale, naked to the sea-winds, at whose bookstalls I bought a publication entitled the *Weekly Telegraph* that contained, week by week, installments of the most thrilling story in the world.

Everywhere romance—the cows moving along the sandy lanes, the sea thundering along the Drigg beach, Gable and Scafell pulling their cloudcaps about their heads, the slow voices of the Cumbrian farmers calling their animals, the little tinkling bell of the Gosforth church—everywhere romance and beauty.

Soon, though, as I became better accustomed to the country, the people immediately around me began to occupy my attention, stimulate my restless curiosity, and especially my two uncles. They were, in fact, queer enough.

Faildyke Hall itself was not queer, only very ugly. It had been built about 1830, I should imagine, a square white building, like a thickset, rather conceited woman, with a very plain face. The rooms were large, the passages innumerable, and everything covered with a very hideous whitewash. Against this whitewash hung old photographs yellowed with age, and faded, bad watercolors. The furniture was strong and ugly.

One romantic feature was the little Gray Tower where my

Uncle Robert lived. This Tower was at the end of the garden and looked out over a sloping field to the Scafell group beyond Wastwater. It had been built hundreds of years ago as a defence against the Scots. Robert had had his study and bedroom there for many years and it was his domain; no one was allowed to enter it save his old servant, Hucking, a bent, wizened, grubby little man who spoke to no one and, so they said in the kitchen, managed to go through life without sleeping. He looked after my Uncle Robert, cleaned his rooms, and was supposed to clean his clothes.

I, being both an inquisitive and romantic-minded boy, was soon as eagerly excited about this Tower as was Bluebeard's wife about the forbidden room. Bob told me that whatever I did I was never to set foot inside.

And then I discovered another thing—that Bob Armstrong hated, feared, and was proud of my Uncle Robert. He was proud of him because he was head of the family, and because, so he said, he was the cleverest old man in the world.

"Nothing he can't seemingly do," said Bob, "but he don't like you to watch him at it."

All this only increased my longing to see the inside of the Tower, although I couldn't be said to be fond of my Uncle Robert either.

It would be hard to say that I disliked him during those first days. He was quite kindly to me when he met me, and at mealtimes, when I sat with my two uncles at the long table in the big, bare, whitewashed dining-room, he was always anxious to see that I had plenty to eat. But I never liked him; it was perhaps because he wasn't clean. Children are sensitive to those things. Perhaps I didn't like the fusty, seedcake-y smell that he carried about with him.

Then there came the day when he invited me into the Gray Tower and told me about Tarnhelm.

Pale slanting shadows of sunlight fell across the chrysanthemums and the gray stone walls, the long fields, and the dusky hills. I was playing by myself by the little stream that ran beyond the rose garden when Uncle Robert came up behind me in the soundless way he had, and, tweaking me by the ear, asked me whether I would like to come with him inside the Tower. I was, of course, eager enough; but I was frightened too, especially when I saw Hucking's moth-eaten old countenance peering at us from one of the narrow slits that pretended to be windows.

However, in we went, my hand in Uncle Robert's hot dry one. There wasn't, in reality, so very much to see when you were inside—all untidy and musty, with cobwebs over the doorways and old pieces of rusty iron and empty boxes in the corners, and the long table in Uncle Robert's study covered with a thousand things—books with the covers hanging on them, sticky green bottles, a looking glass, a pair of scales, a globe, a cage with mice in it, a statue of a naked woman, an hourglass—everything old and stained and dusty.

Uncle Robert made me sit down close to him, and told me many interesting stories. Among others the story about Tarnhelm.

Tarnhelm was something that you put over your head, and its magic turned you into any animal that you wished to be. Uncle Robert told me the story of a god called Wotan, and how he teased the dwarf who possessed Tarnhelm by saying that he couldn't turn himself into a mouse or some such animal; and the dwarf, his pride wounded, turned himself into a mouse, which the god easily captured, and so stole Tarnhelm.

On the table, among all the litter, was a gray skullcap.

"That's *my* Tarnhelm," said Uncle Robert, laughing. "Like to see me put it on?"

But I was suddenly frightened, terribly frightened. The sight of Uncle Robert made me feel quite ill. The room began to run around and around. The white mice in the cage twittered. It was stuffy in that room, enough to turn any boy sick.

[68]

4

That was the moment, I think, when Uncle Robert stretched out his hand towards his gray skullcap; after that I was never happy again in Faildyke Hall. That action of his, simple and apparently friendly though it was, seemed to open my eyes to a number of things.

We were now within ten days of Christmas. The thought of Christmas had then—and, to tell the truth, still has—a most happy effect on me. There is the beautiful story, the geniality and kindliness, still, in spite of modern pessimism, much happiness and goodwill. Even now I yet enjoy giving presents and receiving them—then it was an ecstasy to me, the look of the parcel, the paper, the string, the exquisite surprise.

Therefore I had been anticipating Christmas eagerly. I had been promised a trip into Whitehaven for present-buying, and there was to be a tree and a dance for the Gosforth villagers. Then, after my frightening visit to Uncle Robert's Tower, all my happiness of anticipation vanished. As the days went on and my observation of one thing and another developed, I would, I think, have run away back to my aunts in Kensington had it not been for Bob Armstrong.

It was, in fact, Armstrong who started me on that voyage of observation that ended so horribly, for when he had heard that Uncle Robert had taken me inside his Tower his anger was fearful. I had never before seen him angry; now his great body shook, and he caught me and held me until I cried out.

He wanted me to promise that I would never go inside there again. What? Not even with Uncle Robert? No, most especially *not* with Uncle Robert; and then, dropping his voice and looking around him to be sure that there was no one listening, he began to curse Uncle Robert. This amazed me, because loyalty to his masters was one of Bob's great laws. I can see us now, standing on the stable cobbles in the falling white dusk while the horses stamped in their stalls, and the little sharp stars appeared one after another glittering between the driving clouds.

"I'll not stay," I heard him say to himself. "I'll be like the rest. I'll not be staying. To bring a *child* into it . . ."

From that moment he seemed to have me very specially in his charge. Even when I could not see him I felt that his kindly eye was upon me, and this sense of the necessity that I should be guarded made me yet more uneasy and distressed.

The next thing that I observed was that the servants were all fresh, had been there not more than a month or two. Then, only a week before Christmas, the housekeeper departed. Uncle Constance seemed greatly upset at these occurrences; Uncle Robert did not seem in the least affected by them.

I come now to my Uncle Constance. At this distance of time it is strange with what clarity I still can see him—his stoutness, his shining cleanliness, his dandyism, the flower in his buttonhole, his little brilliantly shod feet, his thin, rather feminine voice. He would have been kind to me, I think, had he dared, but something kept him back. And what that something was I soon discovered; it was fear of my Uncle Robert.

It did not take me a day to discover that he was utterly subject to his brother. He said nothing without looking to see how Uncle Robert took it; suggested no plan until he first had assurance from his brother; was terrified beyond anything that I had before witnessed in a human being at any sign of irritation in my uncle.

I discovered after this that Uncle Robert enjoyed greatly to play on his brother's fears. I did not understand enough of their life to realize what were the weapons that Robert used, but that they were sharp and piercing I was neither too young nor too ignorant to perceive.

Such was our situation, then, a week before Christmas. The weather had become very wild, with a great wind. All nature seemed in an uproar. I could fancy when I lay in my bed at night and heard the shouting in my chimney that I could catch the crash of the waves upon the beach, see the black waters of Wastwater cream and curdle under the Screes. I would lie awake and long for Bob Armstrong—the strength of his arm and the warmth of his breast—but I considered myself too grown a boy to make any appeal.

I remember that now almost minute by minute my fears increased. What gave them force and power who can say? I was much alone. I had now a great terror of my Uncle Robert, the weather was wild, the rooms of the house large and desolate, the servants mysterious, the walls of the passages lit always with an unnatural glimmer because of their white color, and although Armstrong had watch over me he was busy in his affairs and could not always be with me.

I grew to fear and dislike my Uncle Robert more and more. Hatred and fear of him seemed to be everywhere and yet he was always soft-voiced and kindly. Then, a few days before Christmas, occurred the event that was to turn my terror into panic.

I had been reading in the library Mrs. Radcliffe's *Romance of the Forest,* an old book long forgotten, worthy of revival. The library was a fine room run to seed, bookcases from floor to ceiling, the windows small and dark, holes in the old faded carpet. A lamp burned at a distant table. One stood on a little shelf at my side.

Something, I know not what, made me look up. What I saw then can even now stamp my heart in its recollection. By the library door, not moving, staring across the room's length at me, was a yellow dog.

I will not attempt to describe all the pitiful fear and mad freezing terror that caught and held me. My main thought, I fancy, was that that other vision on my first night in the place had not been a dream. I was not asleep now; the book which I had been reading had fallen to the floor, the lamps shed their glow. I could hear the ivy tapping on the pane. No, this was reality.

The dog lifted a long, horrible leg and scratched itself. Then very slowly and silently across the carpet it came towards me.

I could not scream. I could not move; I waited. The animal

was even more evil than it had seemed before, with its flat head, its narrow eyes, its yellow fangs. It came steadily in my direction, stopped once to scratch itself again, then was almost at my chair.

It looked at me, bared its fangs, but now as though it grinned at me, then passed on. After it was gone there was a thick foetid scent in the air—the scent of caraway seed.

5

I think now on looking back that it was remarkable enough that I, a nervous child who trembled at every sound, should have met the situation as I did. I said nothing about the dog to any living soul, not even to Bob Armstrong. I hid my fears—and fears of a beastly and sickening kind they were, too—within my breast. I had the intelligence to perceive—and how I caught in the air the awareness of this I can't, at this distance, understand—that I was playing my little part in the climax to something that had been piling up, for many a month, like the clouds over Gable.

Understand that I offer from first to last in this no kind of explanation. There is possibly—and to this day I cannot quite be sure—nothing to explain. My Uncle Robert died simply—but you shall hear.

What was beyond any doubt or question was that it was after my seeing the dog in the library that Uncle Robert changed so strangely in his behavior to me. That may have been the merest coincidence. I only know that as one grows older one calls things coincidence more and more seldom.

In any case, that same night at dinner Uncle Robert seemed twenty years older. He was bent, shrivelled, would not eat, snarled at anyone who spoke to him, and especially avoided even looking at me. It was a painful meal, and it was after it, when Uncle Constance and I were sitting alone in the old yellow-papered drawing-room—a room with two ticking clocks forever racing one another—that the most extraordinary thing occurred. Uncle Constance and I were playing draughts. The only sounds were the roaring of the wind down the chimney, the hiss and splutter of the fire, the silly ticking of the clocks. Suddenly Uncle Constance put down the piece that he was about to move and began to cry.

To a child it is always a terrible thing to see a grown-up person cry, and even to this day to hear a man cry is very distressing to me. I was moved desperately by poor Uncle Constance, who sat there, his head in his white plump hands, all his stout body shaking. I ran over to him and he clutched me and held me as though he would never let me go. He sobbed incoherent words about protecting me, caring for me . . . seeing that that monster . . .

At the word I remember that I, too, began to tremble. I asked my uncle *what* monster, but he could only continue to murmur incoherently about hate and not having the pluck, and if only he had the courage . . .

Then, recovering a little, he began to ask me questions. Where had I been? Had I been into his brother's Tower? Had I seen anything that frightened me? If I did, would I at once tell him. And then he muttered that he would never have allowed me to come had he known that it would go as far as this, that it would be better if I went away that night, and that if he were not afraid . . . Then he began to tremble again and to look at the door, and I trembled too. He held me in his arms; then we thought that there was a sound, and we listened, our heads up, our two hearts hammering. But it was only the clocks ticking and the wind shrieking as though it would tear the house to pieces.

That night, however, when Bob Armstrong came up to bed he found me sheltering there. I whispered to him that I was frightened; I put my arms around his neck and begged him not to send me away; he promised me that I should not leave him, and I slept all night in the protection of his strength.

How, though, can I give any true picture of the fear that pursued me now? For I knew from what both Armstrong and Uncle Constance had said that there was real danger, that it was no hysterical fancy of mine or ill-digested dream. It made it worse that Uncle Robert was now no more seen. He was sick; he kept within his Tower, cared for by his old wizened manservant. And so, being nowhere, he was everywhere. I stayed with Armstrong when I could, but a kind of pride prevented me from clinging like a girl to his coat.

A deathly silence seemed to fall about the place. No one laughed or sang, no dog barked, no bird sang. Two days before Christmas an iron frost came to grip the land. The fields were rigid, the sky itself seemed to be frozen gray, and under the olive cloud Seafell and Gable were black.

Christmas Eve came.

On that morning, I remember, I was trying to draw—some childish picture of one of Mrs. Radcliffe's scenes—when the double doors unfolded and Uncle Robert stood there. He stood there, bent, shrivelled, his long, gray locks falling over his collar, his bushy eyebrows thrust forward. He wore his old green suit and on his finger gleamed his heavy red ring. I was frightened, of course, but also I was touched with pity. He looked so old, so frail, so small in this large empty house.

I sprang up. "Uncle Robert," I asked timidly, "are you better?"

He bent still lower until he was almost on his hands and feet; then he looked up at me, and his yellow teeth were bared, almost as an animal snarls. Then the doors closed again.

The slow, stealthy, gray afternoon came at last. I walked with Armstrong to Gosforth village on some business that he had. We said no word of any matter at the Hall. I told him, he has reminded me, of how fond I was of him and that I wanted to be with him always, and he answered that perhaps it might be so, little knowing how true that prophecy was to stand. Like all children I had a great capacity for forgetting the atmosphere that I was not at that moment in, and I walked beside Bob along the frozen roads with some of my fears surrendered.

But not for long. It was dark when I came into the long, yellow drawing-room. I could hear the bells of Gosforth church pealing as I passed from the anteroom.

A moment later there came a shrill, terrified cry: "Who's that? Who is it?"

It was Uncle Constance, who was standing in front of the yellow silk curtains, staring at the dusk. I went over to him and he held me close to him.

"Listen," he whispered. "What can you hear?"

The double doors through which I had come were half open. At first I could hear nothing but the clocks, the very faint rumble of a cart on the frozen road. There was no wind.

My uncle's fingers gripped my shoulder. "Listen!" he said again. And now I heard. On the stone passage beyond the drawing-room was the patter of an animal's feet. Uncle Constance and I looked at one another. In that exchanged glance we confessed that our secret was the same. We knew what we should see.

A moment later it was there, standing in the double doorway, crouching a little and staring at us with a hatred that was mad and sick—the hatred of a sick animal crazy with unhappiness, but loathing us more than its own misery.

Slowly it came towards us, and to my fancy all the room seemed to stink of caraway seed.

"Keep back! Keep away!" my uncle screamed.

I became oddly in my turn the protector.

"It shan't touch you! It shan't touch you, uncle!" I called.

But the animal came on.

It stayed for a moment near a little round table that contained a composition of dead waxen fruit under a glass dome. It stayed there, its nose down smelling the ground. Then, looking up at us, it came on again.

Oh God!—even now, as I write after all these years, it is with me again: the flat skull, the cringing body in its evil color, and that loathsome smell. It slobbered a little at its jaw. It bared its fangs.

Then I screamed, hid my face in my uncle's breast, and saw that he held, in his trembling hand, a thick, heavy, old-fashioned revolver.

Then he cried out: "Go back, Robert. . . . Go back!"

The animal came on. He fired. The detonation shook the room. The dog turned, blood dripping from its throat, and crawled across the floor.

By the door it halted, turned, and looked at us. Then it disappeared into the other room.

My uncle had flung down his revolver; he was crying, sniffling; he kept stroking my forehead, murmuring words.

At last, clinging to one another, we followed the splotches of blood, across the carpet, beside the door, through the doorway.

Huddled against a chair in the outer sitting-room, one leg twisted under him, was my Uncle Robert, shot through the throat.

On the floor, by his side, was a gray skullcap.

The Turn of the Tide

C. S. FORESTER

"WHAT ALWAYS BEATS THEM in the end," said Dr. Matthews, "is how to dispose of the body. But, of course, you know that as well as I do."

"Yes," said Slade. He had, in fact, been devoting far more thought to what Dr. Matthews believed to be this accidental subject of conversation than Dr. Matthews could ever guess.

"As a matter of fact," went on Dr. Matthews, warming to the subject to which Slade had so tactfully led him, "it's a terribly knotty problem. It's so difficult, in fact, that I always wonder why anyone is fool enough to commit murder."

All very well for you, thought Slade, but he did not allow his thoughts to alter his expression. *You smug, self-satisfied old fool. You don't know the sort of difficulties a man can be up against.*

"I've often thought the same," he said.

"Yes," went on Dr. Matthews, "it's the body that does it, every time. To use poison calls for special facilities, which are good enough to hang you as soon as suspicion is roused. And that suspicion—well, of course, part of my job is to detect poisoning.

I don't think anyone can get away with it nowadays, even with the most dunderheaded general practitioner."

"I quite agree with you," said Slade. He had no intention of using poison.

"Well," went on Dr. Matthews, developing his logical argument, "if you rule out poison, you rule out the chance of getting the body disposed of under the impression that the victim died a natural death. The only other way, if a man cares to stand the racket of having the body to give evidence against him, is to fake things to look like suicide. But you know, and I know, that it just can't be done.

"The mere fact of suicide calls for a close examination, and no one has ever been able to fix things so well as to get away with it. You're a lawyer. You've probably read a lot of reports on trials where the murderer has tried it on. And you know what's happened to them."

"Yes," said Slade.

He certainly had given a great deal of consideration to the matter. It was only after long thought that he had, finally, put aside the notion of disposing of young Spalding and concealing his guilt by a sham suicide.

"That brings us to where we started, then," said Dr. Matthews. "The only other thing left is to try and conceal the body. And that's more difficult still."

"Yes," said Slade. But he had a perfect plan for disposing of the body.

"A human body," said Dr. Matthews, "is a most difficult thing to get rid of. That chap Oscar Wilde, in that book of his—*Dorian Gray,* isn't it?—gets rid of one by the use of chemicals. Well, I'm a chemist as well as a doctor, and I wouldn't like the job."

"No?" said Slade, politely.

Dr. Matthews was not nearly as clever a man as himself, he thought.

"There's altogether too much of it," said Dr. Matthews. "It's heavy, and it's bulky, and it's bound to undergo corruption. Think of all those poor devils who've tried it. Bodies in trunks, and bodies in coal-cellars, and bodies in chicken-runs. You can't hide the thing, try as you will."

Can't I? That's all you know, thought Slade, but aloud he said: "You're quite right. I've never thought of it before."

"Of course you haven't," agreed Dr. Matthews. "Sensible people don't unless it's an incident of their profession, as in my case."

"And yet you know," he went on, meditatively, "there's one decided advantage about getting rid of the body altogether. You're much safer, then. It's a point which ought to interest you, as a lawyer, more than me. It's rather an obscure point of law, but I fancy there are very definite rulings on it. You know what I'm referring to?"

"No, I don't," said Slade, genuinely puzzled.

"You can't have a trial for murder unless you can prove there's a victim," said Dr. Matthews. "There's got to be a *corpus delicti,* as you lawyers say in your horrible dog-Latin. A corpse, in other words, even if it's only a bit of one, like that which hanged Crippen. No corpse, no trial. I think that's a good law, isn't it?"

"By Jove, you're right!" said Slade. "I wonder why that hadn't occurred to me before?"

No sooner were the words out of his mouth than he regretted having said them. He did his best to make his face immobile again; he was afraid lest his expression might have hinted at his pleasure in discovering another very reassuring factor in this problem of killing young Spalding. But Dr. Matthews had noticed nothing.

"Well, as I said, people only think about these things if they're incidental to their profession," he said. "And, all the same, it's only a theoretical piece of law. The entire destruction of a body is practically impossible. But, I suppose, if a man could achieve it, he would be all right. However strong the suspicion was against him, the police couldn't get him without a corpse. There might be a story in that, Slade, if you or I were writers."

"Yes," assented Slade, and laughed harshly.

There never would be any story about the killing of young Spalding, the insolent pup.

"Well," said Dr. Matthews, "we've had a pretty gruesome conversation, haven't we? And I seem to have done all the talking, somehow. That's the result, I suppose, Slade, of the very excellent dinner you gave me. I'd better push off now. Not that the weather is very inviting."

Nor was it. As Slade saw Dr. Matthews into his car, the rain was driving down in a real winter storm, and there was a bitter wind blowing.

"Shouldn't be surprised if this turned to snow before morning," were Dr. Matthews's last words before he drove off.

Slade was glad it was such a tempestuous night. It meant that, more certainly than ever, there would be no one out in the lanes, no one out on the sands when he disposed of young Spalding's body.

Back in his drawing-room Slade looked at the clock. There was still an hour to spare; he could spend it making sure that his plans were all correct.

He looked up the tide tables. Yes, that was right enough. Spring tides. The lowest of low water on the sands. There was not so much luck about that. Young Spalding came back on the midnight train every Wednesday night, and it was not surprising that, sooner or later, the Wednesday night would coincide with a spring tide. But it was lucky that this particular Wednesday night should be one of tempest; luckier still that low water should be at one-thirty, the best time for him.

He opened the drawing-room door and listened carefully. He could not hear a sound. Mrs. Dumbleton, his housekeeper, must have been in bed some time now. She was as deaf as a post, anyway, and would not hear his departure. Nor his return, when Spalding had been killed and disposed of.

The hands of the clock seemed to be moving very fast. He must make sure everything was correct. The plough chain and the other iron weights were already in the back seat of his car; he had put them there before old Matthews arrived to dine. He slipped on his overcoat.

From his desk, Slade took a curious little bit of apparatus: eighteen inches of strong cord, tied at each end to a six-inch length of wood so as to make a ring. He made a last close examination to see that the knots were quite firm, and then he put it in his pocket: As he did so, he ran through, in his mind, the words—he knew them by heart—of the passage in the book about the thugs of India, describing the method of strangulation employed by them.

He could think quite coldly about all this. Young Spalding was a pestilent busybody. A word from him, now, could bring ruin upon Slade, could send him to prison, could have him struck off the rolls.

Slade thought of other defaulting solicitors he had heard of, even one or two with whom he had come into contact professionally. He remembered his brother-solicitors' remarks about them, pitying or contemptuous. He thought of having to beg his bread in the streets on his release from prison, of cold and misery and starvation. The shudder which shook him was succeeded by a hot wave of resentment. Never, never, would he endure it.

What right had young Spalding, who had barely been qualified two years, to condemn a gray-haired man twenty years his senior to such a fate? If nothing but death would stop him, then he deserved to die. He clenched his hand on the cord in his pocket.

A glance at the clock told him he had better be moving. He

turned out the lights and tiptoed out of the house, shutting the door quietly. The bitter wind flung icy rain into his face, but he did not notice it.

He pushed the car out of the garage by hand, and, contrary to his wont, he locked the garage doors, as a precaution against the infinitesimal chance that, on a night like this, someone should notice that his car was out.

He drove cautiously down the road. Of course, there was not a soul about in a quiet place like this. The few streetlamps were already extinguished.

There were lights in the station as he drove over the bridge: They were awaiting there the arrival of the twelve-thirty train. Spalding would be on that. Every Wednesday he went over to his subsidiary office, sixty miles away. Slade turned into the lane a quarter of a mile beyond the station, and then reversed his car so that it pointed towards the road. He put out the sidelights, and settled himself to wait: His hand fumbled with the cord in his pocket.

The train was a little late. Slade had been waiting a quarter of an hour when he saw the lights of the train emerge from the cutting and come to a standstill in the station. So wild was the night that he could hear nothing of it. Then the train moved slowly out again. As soon as it was gone, the lights in the station began to go out, one by one: Hobson, the porter, was making ready to go home, his turn of duty completed.

Next, Slade's straining ears heard footsteps.

Young Spalding was striding down the road. With his head bent before the storm, he did not notice the dark mass of the motorcar in the lane, and he walked past it.

Slade counted up to two hundred slowly, and then he switched on the lights, started the engine, and drove the car out into the road in pursuit. He saw Spalding in the light of the headlamps and drew up alongside.

"Is that Spalding?" he said, striving to make the tone of his voice as natural as possible. "I'd better give you a lift, old man, hadn't I?"

"Thanks very much," said Spalding. "This isn't the sort of night to walk two miles in."

He climbed in and shut the door. No one had seen. No one would know. Slade let his clutch out and drove slowly down the road.

"Bit of luck, seeing you," he said. "I was just on my way home from bridge at Mrs. Clay's when I saw the train come in and remembered it was Wednesday and you'd be walking home. So I thought I'd turn a bit out of my way to take you along."

"Very good of you, I'm sure," said Spalding.

"As a matter of fact," said Slade, speaking slowly and driving slowly, "it wasn't altogether disinterested. I wanted to talk business to you, as it happened."

"Rather an odd time to talk business," said Spalding. "Can't it wait till tomorrow?"

"No, it cannot," said Slade. "It's about the Lady Vere trust."

"Oh, yes. I wrote to remind you last week that you had to make delivery?"

"Yes, you did. And I told you, long before that, that it would be inconvenient, with Hammond abroad."

"I don't see that," said Spalding. "I don't see that Hammond's got anything to do with it. Why can't you just hand over and have done with it? I can't do anything to straighten things up until you do."

"As I said, it would be inconvenient."

Slade brought the car to a standstill at the side of the road.

"Look here, Spalding," he said desperately. "I've never asked a favor of you before. But now I ask you, as a favor, to forgo delivery for a bit, just for three months, Spalding."

But Slade had small hope that his request would be granted. So little hope, in fact, that he brought his left hand out of his pocket holding the piece of wood, with the loop of cord dangling

[83]

from its ends. He put his arm around the back of Spalding's seat.

"No, I can't, really I can't," said Spalding. "I've got my duty to my clients to consider. I'm sorry to insist, but you're quite well aware of what my duty is."

"Yes," said Slade, "but I beg of you to wait. I implore you to wait, Spalding. There! Perhaps you can guess why, now."

"I see," said Spalding, after a long pause.

"I only want three months," pressed Slade. "Just three months. I can get straight again in three months."

Spalding had known other men who had had the same belief in their ability to get straight in three months. It was unfortunate for Slade—and for Spalding—that Slade had used those words. Spalding hardened his heart.

"No," he said. "I can't promise anything like that. I don't think it's any use continuing this discussion. Perhaps I'd better walk home from here."

He put his hand to the latch of the door, and, as he did so, Slade jerked the loop of cord over his head. A single turn of Slade's wrist—a thin, bony, old man's wrist, but as strong as steel in that wild moment—tightened the cord about Spalding's throat.

Slade swung around in his seat, getting both hands to the piece of wood, twisting madly. His breath hissed between his teeth with the effort, but Spalding never drew breath at all. He lost consciousness long before he was dead. Only Slade's grip of the cord around his throat prevented the dead body from falling forward, doubled up.

Nobody had seen, nobody would know. And what that book had stated about the method of assassination practised by thugs was perfectly correct.

Slade had gained, now, the time in which he could get his affairs in order. With all the promise of his current speculations, with all his financial ability, he would be able to recoup himself for his past losses. It only remained to dispose of Spalding's body, and he had planned to do that very satisfactorily. Just for a moment Slade felt as if all this were only some heated dream, some nightmare, but then he came back to reality and went on with the plan he had in mind.

He pulled the dead man's knees forward so that the corpse lay back in the seat, against the side of the car. He put the car in gear, let out his clutch, and drove rapidly down the road—much faster than when he had been arguing with Spalding. Low water was in three-quarters of an hour's time, and the sands were ten miles away.

Slade drove fast through the wild night. There was not a soul about in those lonely lanes. He knew the way by heart, for he had driven repeatedly over that route recently in order to memorize it.

The car bumped down the last bit of lane, and Slade drew up on the edge of the sands.

It was pitch dark, and the bitter wind was howling about him under the black sky. Despite the noise of the wind, he could hear the surf breaking far away, two miles away, across the level sands. He climbed out of the driver's seat and walked around to the other door. When he opened it the dead man fell sideways, into his arms.

With an effort, Slade held him up while he groped into the back of the car for the plough chain and the iron weights. He crammed the weights into the dead man's clothes, tucking in the ends to make it all secure. With that mass of iron to hold it down, the body would never be found again when dropped into the sea at the lowest ebb of the spring tide.

Slade tried now to lift the body in his arms, to carry it over the sands. He reeled and strained, but he was not strong enough— Slade was a man of slight figure and past his prime. The sweat on his forehead was icy in the cold wind.

For a second, doubts overwhelmed him, lest all his plans should fail for want of bodily strength. But he forced himself into thinking clearly—forced his frail body into obeying the vehement commands of his brain.

He turned around, still holding the dead man upright. Stooping, he got the heavy burden on his shoulders. He drew the arms around his neck, and, with a convulsive effort, he got the legs up around his hips. The dead man now rode him pig-a-back. Bending nearly double, he was able to carry the heavy weight in that fashion, the arms tight around his neck, the legs tight around his waist.

He set off, staggering down the imperceptible slope of the sands towards the sound of the surf. The sands were soft beneath his feet. It was because of this softness that he had not driven the car down to the water's edge. He could afford to take no chances of being embogged.

The icy wind shrieked around him all that long way. The tide was nearly two miles out. That was why Slade had chosen this place. In the depth of winter, no one would go out to the water's edge at low tide for months to come.

He staggered on over the sands, clasping the limbs of the body close about him. Desperately, he forced himself forward, not stopping to rest, for he only had time now to reach the water's edge before the flow began. He went on and on, driving his exhausted body with fierce urgings from his frightened brain.

Then, at last, he saw it: a line of white in the darkness which indicated the water's edge. Farther out, the waves were breaking in an inferno of noise. Here, the fragments of the rollers were only just sufficient to move the surface a little.

He was going to make quite sure of things. Steadying himself, he stepped into the water, wading in farther and farther so as to be able to drop the body into comparatively deep water. He held to his resolve, staggering through the icy water, knee-deep, thigh-deep, until it was nearly at his waist. This was far enough. He stopped, gasping in the darkness.

He leaned over to one side, to roll the body off his back. It did not move. He pulled at its arms. They were obstinate. He could not loosen them. He shook himself wildly. He tore at the legs around his waist. Still the thing clung to him. Wild with panic and fear, he flung himself about in a mad effort to rid himself of the burden. It clung on as though it were alive. He could not break its grip, no matter how hard he tried.

Then another breaker came in. It splashed about him, wetting him far above his waist. The tide had begun to turn now, and the tide on those sands comes in like a racehorse.

He made another effort to cast off the load, and, when it still held him fast, he lost his nerve and tried to struggle out of the sea. But it was too much for his exhausted body. The weight of the corpse and of the iron with which it was loaded overbore him. He fell.

He struggled up again in the foam-streaked, dark sea, staggered a few steps, fell again—and did not rise. The dead man's arms were around his neck, throttling him, strangling him. Rigor mortis had set in and Spalding's muscles had refused to relax.

Fear

P. C. WREN

1

FROM THE FIRST MOMENT I disliked the bungalow intensely.
Nor had this feeling anything to do with the fact that it was
dirty, derelict, and tumbledown; nor, again, that it was lonely,
isolated, and obviously long uninhabited.

It was the atmosphere, aura, the spirit of the house that was
antipathetic, inimical. Even outside it, one had this feeling of an
emanated antagonism. Inside, the feeling deepened, and one
seemed conscious almost of warning; and then of danger; and
finally, of threat.

I was reminded of that remarkable and haunting line which
once he has read it, occasionally returns to the mind of the
traveler in little-visited and out-of-the-way corners of the earth:

The place was silent and—aware.

Certainly this place was silent, and undoubtedly one had an
uneasy feeling of its awareness, of being watched, of being

expected—and unwelcome. Not watched by human eyes, but by the place itself.

It was an old—and old-fashioned—rest-house, built on *teangs*, strong square pillars, some twelve feet in height, of *meribau* wood, that hard red wood which is proof against the attack of insects, including even the white ant.

Mounting the flight of steps that led up to the platform on which the house was built, and entering the big central room, the thought immediately entered my mind that "rest-house" was a misnomer. I felt quite certain that whatever else I got here, I should get little rest.

I had frequently been in places which gave the impression that the *genius loci* was inimical. I had been conscious of the feeling, both in buildings made by hands and in places but rarely trodden by human foot; in certain swamps, canyons, dark forests, caves, and sun-blasted or wind-harried desert places.

I have had this feeling strongly when spending a dark and lonely night in Angkor Wat; and again in the brilliant sunlight of a beautiful morning on top of the hill called Doi Wieng Lek, a hill situated near Lampang, in Siam. *Doi Wieng Lek* means "the hill which is the place of evil spirit," a fact of which I was unaware, or at any rate, did not realize, until I had left it.

But standing on top of the hill, which I had climbed in order to admire a view of the Lampang plain and the distant hills, I was suddenly conscious of an uneasiness, which was but little removed from fear. What caused the uneasiness, and of what I should be afraid, when mental discomfort and apprehensiveness deepened into fear, I had not the slightest idea. It had nothing to do with the fact that practically every tree looked as though it had been struck by lightning, which certainly was not the case. It was not that I heard any of those sounds which, in certain places, are perturbing, if not startling; it was not because the trees seemed to have been deserted by both birds and gibbons, in spite of the fact that all the surrounding jungle was alive with the gibbons, little spidery long-armed long-legged monkeys whose bewhiskered faces are so friendly and amusing, and whose call is musical, yet so mournful. . . .

But the house.

I am not psychic. I am not a nervous person nor sensitive, I am not fanciful, superstitious, nor suggestible; but, like everybody else who is not an absolute clod, I have a sense of atmosphere, whether it be social or local. And never in my life have I been so quickly or so strongly aware of an eerie and minatory atmosphere as in this abandoned rest-house. Had it been possible, I would have marched on, and left it to its loneliness and gloom. For I felt it was haunted, tragic, and evil. However, I had no choice. Here I was, and here, for a period, I must remain. For, however unpleasant the place might be, to flee from it and return, the object of my journey unaccomplished, would have been more so. I should have felt ashamed of myself. Also ridiculous. For how could I possibly explain that I had found the place, according to directions given me by kindly hosts in Muzlongse, had not entered into possession, but had simply fled, frightened away.

It seemed to me that my coolies disliked the place almost as much as I did, for with unwonted rapidity they unpacked the *hahps,* the big baskets made of woven bamboo, which hang at either end of a pole balanced over the shoulder, and in which one's food, clothes, and other chattels are transported in that part of the world.

Nor did my jungle guide appear disposed to linger, when once he had set up my camp-bed and served my dinner, a remarkably well-cooked and satisfying meal, consisting principally of a stew of tinned meat, rice, alleged mushrooms, bamboo shoots, dough-dumplings, chillies, and unidentifiable odds and ends.

In view of the fact that my cook had, so far as I knew, neither materials nor apparatus for cooking, the effort was beyond praise.

Having dined, I carried my collapsible chair out onto the verandah, lit a cigarette—and told myself not to be a fool. For I felt more uncomfortable, more lonely, more apprehensive than ever before in all my life.

From where I sat, the moonlit jungle looked beautiful—but unfriendly, threatening; and the danger implicit in the threat was not from the leopard or the tiger.

Generally speaking, this was one of the best hours of the day, the march completed, dinner eaten, and a pleasant tiredness enhancing the flavor of tobacco and the enjoyment of a book. A good hour for the review of the events of the day, the making of plans for the morrow, and appreciation of one's good fortune in being so far from the madding crowd and the din of an increasingly clamorous civilization.

The ocean, the desert, and the jungle are the last strongholds and resorts of peace.

But here there was no peace. Silence, so far as the jungle is ever silent; utter stillness; but no peace—of mind.

Decidedly this was a bad place, or else I was going to be ill. It must be that. . . . Fever . . . Liver . . . And yet, until I came within sight of this derelict house, I had been in perfect health.

I had better go to bed.

Reentering the big central room, on either side of which were two bedrooms, I turned up the wick of the lamp that hung from a roof-beam, and took stock of the place. What immediately caught my attention and gave me a slight shock of surprise was the fact that, across one corner of the room, was a piano.

Now, I have had a perhaps unusually wide experience of rest-houses, *dak* bungalows, *pahugs,* and such buildings, provided for the shelter of the casual traveler in India, Ceylon, Burma, Siam, Malaya, Annam, Cambodia, and certain parts of Africa and China; but never yet have I discovered one provided with a piano. I have known them to be well-fitted, well-kept houses, with one or more resident servants; and I have known them to be dirty derelict huts, with one or more resident reptiles, poisonous, domiciled, and waiting—but never a piano.

And as my eye roamed around the ill-lit room, I discovered that it differed, in other respects, from the usual central hall common to the use of travelers occupying the different bedrooms —should more than one traveler be occupying the rest-house at the same time.

Such a room generally contains a dining-table and four chairs.

This room was furnished; and old, neglected, tattered, dust-covered, and derelict as the furniture might be, it had once been drawing-room furniture. There was what had been a handsome screen at each door; there were a sofa and armchairs; pictures had once adorned the walls, and the cracked, dirty, and insect-riddled remains still hung in their places. In a teak-wood bookcase were the remains of books, now the home of the fish-insect, the ant, the cockroach, and the rat. In a corner was a standard lamp, about whose glass chimney and globe still hung the tattered remnants of a silk shade. And beneath my feet was a matting of a very different quality from that of the usual plaited palm-leaf to be found in the ordinary travelers' rest-house. This was of fine Chinese reed-work and had cost money.

And incongruous, in this ghost of a long-dead drawing-room, stood a bed. Beside it, my jungle guide had set up my own folding camp-bed, which looked neat, clean, and positively attractive beside the much bigger one, once comparatively sumptuous, now a dubious-looking mass of discolored, dust-covered silk and grimy linen.

Here and there a gleam of color showed through dust which lay so thickly as to amount almost to a covering of earth or ash. Part of this, of course, would be the settling dust of years, part a precipitate of fine bamboo and other wood sawdust that had rained down upon it from the roof and rafters above, as the boring insects proceeded with their uninterrupted labors of destruction.

A truly dreadful room, suggesting to my mind an aged crone dressed in finery that she had worn for fifty years; a hag, evil and malignant, foul and filthy, yet not only alive, but retaining, beneath the dirt of ages, faint rare glimpses of a former finery.

But why sleep in this drawing-room of a nightmare, when there were apparently four bedrooms opening from this central room?

On a bedside table—who last had used that bedside table, and had it been a man or a woman?—I saw that my guide had placed my Hitchcock lamp, one of those invaluable pieces of camp-furniture, which, needing neither chimney nor globe, gives an excellent if fierce light, and whose loud and insistent ticking is something that soothes or maddens the nerves of the lonely listener, according to the state of his mind, or more probably of his liver.

Picking it up, I lit it, and opened the nearest door.

In this room were two beds, a leg-rest chair, and a dressing-table with mirror. The room was in some disorder, and was evidently exactly as it had been left by its last occupants when, hurriedly, they departed.

Returning to the drawing-room and closing the door behind me, I entered the other room on the same side, and discovered similar conditions. This, also, was a double bedroom, or at any rate a room last occupied by two people, the almost moldering remains of tumbled bedding, and suggestions of hurried departure, if not sudden flight.

And similarly in the case of the two other bedrooms.

Eight guests—and a ninth person, the host, who had slept in the drawing-room that fatal night, had fled in haste, leaving everything as it stood.

Having made my tour of inspection, I sat down in a spacious armchair—and almost went through it to the floor. For one hideous moment of imprisonment I struggled in a position of great indignity and extreme discomfort, until I contrived to extricate myself from what was really a very neat trap.

"Good heavens!" thought I, as at length, breathless, I got to my feet and surveyed the now bottomless chair, "I might have stuck there till I died," the idiotic thought being in keeping with my frame of mind and my environment. For I should hardly have died before morning, when my guide and the coolies would have come. On the other hand, in that horrible position, with my knees firmly pressed against my chest, I might very well have died of suffocation, heart failure, or of a broken blood-vessel.

And once again, what rubbish, when my heart was as strong as that of a horse, and my arteries as soft as india rubber. And yet, fear, horror, and despair are not ridiculous; and, for a few seconds, while firmly wedged into that malevolent-seeming chair, endowed with devilish intention, I had been frightened, horrified, and despairing of ever escaping from the trap.

However, fear had its usual reaction, anger, and I felt thoroughly and savagely annoyed—a much healthier mental state.

I would undress and go to bed; and the devil and all his imps could play any game they fancied, in, around, above, and below the bungalow; and I would not so much as open an eye and cast a glance at them.

So I thought, or at any rate, so I told myself, and raising the mosquito-curtain, got into bed, tucked the edge of the curtain in, turned the light down very low, closed my eyes, and composed myself for sleep.

Suddenly, something creaked very loudly. I opened my eyes and sat up; and sleep fled further from me than ever.

This wouldn't do. If I were going to jump up like that every time there was a creak, I should spend a restless night. But this had been no ordinary creak; and lest it should seem strange and unreasonable that one should differentiate between one creak and another, I will mention that the sound was precisely that which I myself had made in walking across the wooden floor.

As I have said, the bungalow was supported upon *teangs,* great posts which raised it some twelve feet above the ground, and the floor was of boards, one or two of which, probably owning to shrinkage in dry weather after being swollen during the rains, creaked quite audibly when trodden on, somewhat as do the stairs in all old houses.

I was perfectly certain that someone, probably a bare-footed native, had crossed the room.

Hastily pulling out the linen border of the mosquito-curtain from under the thin mattress of the camp-bed, I turned up the lamp.

The room was empty, of course, and as I perfectly well knew.

Neither my jungle guide nor any coolie would come into the room before dawn, and no dacoit would wander about in that fashion, within a minute of my getting into bed. What a dacoit would do would be to creep up the steps, glide like a ghost—damn that word *ghost!*—across the verandah, and with a rush and a leap, drive his *kris* through my throat.

Or so I argued.

Anyway, there was nobody in the room. Nobody visible, that is to say.

And again I turned down the lamp, tucked in the mosquito-curtain, turned on to my right side, firmly closed my eyes, and prayed the old English prayer.

> *From bogles and bugaboos, warlocks and warricoes,*
> *Ghaisties and ghoulies, long-leggity beasties,*
> *And things that go wump in the night,*
> *Good Lord, deliver us.*

I closed my eyes but unfortunately I could not close my ears, and the loud creak that was obviously made by someone stepping upon one of those loose boards again sounded through the room, sudden and sharp as the crack of a pistol. That was a gross exaggeration, of course. It was more like the snapping of a twig beneath the unpracticed foot in the dry jungle, the tiny resounding snap that warns the stalked prey of the approach of heavy-footed clumsy death—or murder most foul but self-defeated.

For some reason, or for no reason, I suddenly remembered my Irish batman and his favorite formula for use on all occasions. "Ah, to Hell wit' it, then!"

That was the proper attitude of mind and the suitable incantation.

Again the sound of stealthy footsteps.

Bosh! That was an absolute boys' magazine cliché. There was no sound of footsteps, stealthy or otherwise—only the noise of someone treading on loose boards.

But surely a ghost, a spirit, a *bhut, afrit, peh,* was imponderable, without substance, and quite incapable of depressing a warped board.

It wasn't incapable of depressing me, though, and my possibly warped mind.

A loud creak, as someone or something—or nothing—trod on another place where a board under the matting responded beneath the pressure.

"Ah, to Hell wit' it!"

And then, almost with a shriek, I again sprang bolt upright, for a pair of giant hands, with fingers spread from end to end of the keyboard, crashed down upon the keys of the piano, bringing forth a terrific and hideous cacophony, a horrible jangling discord, discernible through which were the sounds of breaking wires.

Good God! Angels and ministers of grace defend us!

I admit that it was with a hand decidedly inclined to tremble that I again turned up the light, and saw that there was no one at the piano, or in the room.

But really, this would not do. This was not only beyond a joke, it was beyond all reason. Clearly and definitely it was beyond reason that invisible hands should strike a crashing chord upon a piano.

I'm sure there are brave men who would have said "Tut, tut!" Possibly have walked to the piano, played a hymn-tune— "Eternal Father, strong to save," perhaps—and returned to bed the better for the performance.

Personally, I was much more inclined to get well down under the clothes, pull them over my head, and stay there till a cold or bony hand removed them.

What I did do was to sit and stare, wide-eyed and open-mouthed, while I burst into a cold sweat and tried to find rational explanation for the astonishing—and indeed in that place, at that hour, appalling—phenomenon.

The creaking of the loose boards I could explain away, more or less—in point of fact, very much less—satisfactorily, by remembering how furniture creaks, and indeed bangs, occasionally, in old houses, in the middle of the night. (Though why the devil it should always choose the middle of the night for that exercise is something of a mystery.)

The boards might creak and groan without having been trodden upon by human or nonhuman foot; it might be their playful habit and old-established custom to wait till midnight and then make precisely the noise they made when a heavy man stepped on them.

But what about the piano? I could not remember ever previously having slept in the same room as a piano, but I was prepared to wager a very large sum that though the woodwork of an aged and neglected piano might conceivably utter a creak or, through the sudden breaking of a wire, emit a doleful jangling *ping,* it could not possibly produce a hellish uproar in which a score of keys and strings were concerned.

I was prepared to admit that in the lonely stillness of the most ordinary drawing-room in the most commonplace bungalow, a piano, through the slipping of a wire, might make one unmusical sound; but it was inconceivable that it should make a hundred hideous jangling noises.

Cursing my cowardice, I turned the light right out.

Staring into the darkness, I could see nothing; and this is not so much a statement of the obvious as it sounds, for the darkness was not complete, not that darkness as of black velvet. The night without was lit by a gibbous moon and the brilliant tropic stars.

No, I could see nothing. But again someone at the piano played a rough and violent discord.

Raising my mosquito-curtain, I struck a match and lit the table-lamp. As I did so, I heard a heavy thud, followed by minor movements.

Lifting the lamp above my head with a hand undoubtedly beginning to tremble, I looked around the room. There was nothing whatsoever to be seen, save the decrepit furniture.

"Another little smoke wouldn't do us any harm," said I aloud, to show myself how bold a fellow of yet-unshaken nerve was I.

Something rustled in reply.

"Rats!" said I. "Rats. And this can be taken as a reference to rodents or as a derisive ejaculation." Which statement, made solemnly and aloud, showed me that, whatever I might pretend, I was nervous. I would get up, light the hanging lamp, turn the small one up, and read until daylight.

No—damned if I would. For the rest of my life I should be ashamed to look myself in the face.

I finished my cigarette, turned out my lamp again, and, as a concession to human frailty and cowardice, took the matches into bed with me, tucked in the mosquito-curtain, and composed myself to slumber.

Never yet have I found any of the devices advocated for sleep-inducement of the slightest effect or value. Speaking for myself, the only thing is to relax, mind and body, beginning with the muscles of the toes and working up to those of the scalp, consciously relaxing and letting go all holds, one after the other, and finally making the mind a blank—or blanker than usual.

I had worked my way up to the arms, and had just made my hands and forearms utterly inert, when there was what might be called—and indeed must be called, for there is no other description—"a ghastly cry." And the ghastly cry was uttered within the room.

It was something between a moan, a wail, and a scream. I struck a match. It broke, fell onto the bedclothes, and went out. And in the brief half-second of light, I saw what again might be called—indeed must be called, for there is no other description —"something white," a ghostly figure that crossed the room.

I struck another match, pulled up the mosquito-curtain with a great air of resolution and determination to look into the matter and do something, only to discover that there was no matter into which to look, and nothing to be done. There was no sound in the room, and certainly there was no "something white."

"And this is where another little drink wouldn't do us any harm," said I.

In point of fact, it had no opportunity to do any harm or any good, for I had nothing to drink save a little soda-water in the bottle left by my jungle guide. There was not even the *nam tohn* of porous clay with a tin cup inverted over its neck, usually to be found in *dak* bungalows; and, had there been one, I should have hesitated to drink from it. Why, it is difficult to say. What is the difference between germ-infested water brought straight from the nearest *huey* or pond to the bungalow, and water of the native-owned soda-water shop? Of the two, perhaps the soda-water is the more dangerous, as its inhabitant microbes must be in a higher state of stimulation and activity—not to mention the mud and other filth encrusted in the neck of the soda-water bottle.

Having decided, I drank the soda-water and lay down, after noting that, according to my watch, the night was still young, the hour being but two o'clock. Well, plenty of time for plenty of doings.

Soon I fell asleep—even as do men who await the dawn firing-party or the gaol officials who come to lead them to the scaffold. In that cheery frame of mind.

Anyhow, I must have slept, because undoubtedly I was

awakened. How much of what I experienced in the act of awakening was dream, how much imagination, and how much an utterly unreal reality, I don't know, but I do know that from a dream or from dreamless sleep I awoke to the knowledge that there was a party in progress in the room. I must have been in the act of opening my eyes as I saw lights, the forms of men, heard speech and laughter; and what is more, noticed that it was slurred speech and overnoisy laughter.

So certain was I of this, that, in the moment of sitting up and going to raise my mosquito-curtain once more, the feeling uppermost in my mind was one of indignation. What right had these fellows to come carousing and bingeing in my room at three or four o'clock in the morning? A most disgusting exhibition of caddish ill-manners, and I threw up the curtain, prepared to speak my mind to that effect.

Of course there were no bright lights; there was no sound of revelry by night.

But there *was*. . . .

They were trooping down the steps from the verandah to the garden. And as for a second I listened, now terrified rather than indignant, I knew that the merry party, instead of spreading itself over the garden with joyous whoops, drunken shouts, and alcoholic song, turned in under the bungalow among the *teangs,* pillars of *meribau* wood that supported the house.

Distinctly I heard them. Distinctly I heard a crash, as of something heavy overturned. Distinctly I heard shouts and cries which were not merry nor amusing; and, finally, a sound such as I hope never to hear again. Those who have heard the scream of a wounded horse will have some idea of the bloodcurdling horror of that dreadful cry, a clear-cut shocking shriek that seemed to freeze the marrow of my bones and cause the hair of my head to stand on end.

I had had enough.

Getting out of bed and pulling on my boots, I lit the Hitchcock lamp, turned it up until its flame was as high as it would go, and was thankful for its steady brilliance, and the fact that it needed neither globe nor chimney, which might have blackened and broken and obscured the light.

And holding high my lamp, I crossed the verandah, descended the steps and boldly—yes, boldly!—plunged into the midst of whatever might be happening in the pillared gloom of the dreadful place beneath the bungalow.

For it *was* dreadful.

Not because of anything that was there, but because there was *nothing* there. No sign or sound of human being, animal, ghost, or spirit briefly incarnate.

Save for the fact that it had no outer walls, the place was like a crypt, the big baulks of timber that supported the house suggesting Norman pillars of stone. Several feet above my head were the boards of the floor of the room from which I had just come. Beneath my feet was what had been hard-beaten earth, now in parts thinly covered by sickly weeds. No sign whatsoever of human visitation or occupation was there, save the collapsed timbers of what had been a big packing-case.

I was defeated, and promptly and willingly admitting defeat, fled from the place, mounted the steps, and reentered my bed-drawing-room.

Compared with the cellarlike place beneath the house, this horrible and haunted room seemed almost attractive; for inimical as was its atmosphere, it was not as fear-compelling as the other.

Here above, I felt fear. There below, I felt a horror and a terror fearful beyond fear.

A return to bed, somnolence, and an attitude of defenceless acquiescence were out of the question, and I began to dress, involuntarily glancing over my shoulder, swiftly turning about to see what was behind me, as I did so.

And on this occasion, as not infrequently before, I was glad that I was an extremely temperate person, and that for me, alcohol had no attraction. (Incidentally, I really do not make this idiosyncrasy a cause for any self-approval. If I liked alcohol I should drink it.) I was glad because all that I had heard and the little I had seen really *had* been heard and seen. There was no question of it. It was no alcohol-induced or drug-begotten fantasy. I had heard sounds when wide awake, as widely awake as I was now, dressing.

True, I had awakened suddenly to see lights and hear sounds that might have been part of a dream; but I felt absolutely convinced that they had also been part of waking experience.

Well, "There are more things in Heaven and earth . . ."

And whether I had been imagining things, dreaming dreams, and seeing visions, or not, one thing was certain: Nothing on earth, absolutely nothing, would induce me to spend another night in this place; nay nor another hour more than was necessary for my getting away from it.

2

Next night I camped in the jungle, a most unpleasant night of wind and rain and conditions that defeated even my accomplished Lao cook and jungle guide. A night that should have been memorable for its acute and complicated discomfort, but which, in point of fact, is memorable for its sweet peacefulness, a sweetness unsoured by cold driving rain and devilish plucking wind, a peace unbroken by the heaviest crashes of violent thunderstorms. Sweetness and peace, because this was the jungle, and not that fear-stricken, horror-infested bungalow.

What were tigers, leopards, king cobras, scorpions, leeches— and the greatest of these is leeches—compared with one sound, one sight, in that house of dread?

The following night I slept in a *Wat.*

We reached it at sundown, and it had an air of solid comfort very reassuring to me after what I had been through. It was but a small *Wat* situated at the end of a green path which led to it from the road, a distance of about two hundred yards. Its outer court or hall of stone was clean and had a well-cared-for air about it. This outer hall had no walls and its stone roof was supported on four heavy stone pillars. Near the entrance was an ancient sacred *Boh*-tree whose branches were so heavy that each one had to be supported by a pole resting on the earth.

The *Wat* was empty save for one *poogni* in a yellow robe, who was chanting before the stone image of Buddha, and he took no notice of me, until, presently departing, he gave me the usual greeting of *"Sabai-ga?"* (Are you well?), to which I answered the usual *"Sabai!"* Quite well).

In front of the enormous effigy of the Buddha were arranged the heterogeneous collection of offerings which are usually to be found in these *Wats* and which never cease to astonish me, by reason of their strange variety.

There were stone jam-jars containing dead flowers, cheap alarm-clocks, such as are found in the village-shops in England, bunches of dried flowers, brightly colored feathers, celluloid or glass balls, bits of colored china, tin, and enamel mugs. There were also numerous candles stuck in the melted wax of others long-since burnt out. These candles are lit only at festival times, when the villagers come to make their offerings.

Here in this place was Peace, for over it brooded the spirit of the Buddha, beneficent, well-wishing; and the pious founder of the temple had been one who fain would acquire merit.

In it I slept peacefully.

On the next day my guide, leading our little party, suddenly turned aside and took a path even narrower and fainter than that on which we were. Some little distance down this path was a bamboo *pahng* or *sala,* built in a clearing in the jungle. It is not unusual to find these shelters in various parts of the dense forests. They were quite unfurnished and empty, and may be used by any passing traveler who happens to know where they are situated. The walls and floor are made of split bamboo. While perfectly strong and adequate, the bamboo floor is apt to be rather disconcerting when one walks on one of them for the first time, for it springs up and down with every movement, and it is difficult to keep one's balance until one becomes accustomed to the feeling of walking on springs.

This particular *pahng* was very charmingly situated. Behind it rose a steep hillside covered with small teak-trees which were in flower. There were also many shrubs, with leaves of various shades of red and gold. In front of the *pahng* was the clearing, beyond which were the tall trees of the forest, and growing up one side of the shelter itself was a thick bush of the pale pink Honolulu creeper which someone had, at some time or other, planted there.

Here again I slept in peace, and on the following night reached the house of an American medical missionary.

The Reverend Dr. Gates proved to be a most interesting man, the soul of hospitality, as unlike the missionary of nitwit fiction as a man could be; and most definitely a doctor, an ethnologist, botanist, zoologist, and general scientist long before he was a parson. When, purely for the sake of making conversation, a thing that at first has to be made when one meets a man who has not spoken his own language for months or years, I somewhat fatuously asked him if he had made many converts, he somewhat disconcertingly replied:

"Converts to what?" and later admitted modestly that he had possibly converted a few wild Was to tameness, a few Karens and possibly one or two arboreal Mois to elementary ideas of hygiene and handicraft.

Anyhow, shy jungle-folk came to him with their wives and other troubles, realizing that his methods of *accouchement* were better than those of their own witch-doctors, who did not invariably get the best results from their methods.

After an excellent dinner that night, we settled down to talk, and, having lived long enough to know when the most successful conversationalist is he who uses his ears far more than his mouth, I got the doctor to tell me of his life's work.

And when the good doctor at length fell silent, after apologizing for having talked so much, and I had told him it was the best talk I had had for years, I introduced the subject that, even so, was uppermost in my mind.

"Do you believe in ghosts, Doctor?" I asked as he stuffed his pipe.

"Ghosts," he laughed. "Depends entirely on what you *mean* by ghosts. I haven't an unshakable belief in the chain-rattling figure of the wicked Sir Giles who crosses the moonlit hall at midnight; nor much in the Gray Lady who is discovered sitting in costume in the music room at sunset on Saint John's Eve. . . . Why? Do you believe in ghosts?"

"Depends entirely on what you mean by ghosts," I smiled. "I didn't believe in any sort of kind of ghost until last Monday night. Now I have to do so."

"Last Monday night. Let's see. Four marches back. Ah! That means the abandoned bungalow just over the border, the one they tried to turn into a rest-house. Stayed a night there, did you? What happened?"

"Oh, a lot of funny things. First of all, a ghost walked up and down the room in the silence and the darkness—breaking the stillness of the night by causing the boards to creak beneath his weight."

"The weight of a ghost!" smiled the doctor.

"Weight of something," I said.

"Well, deal with that first. Suppose a leopard came in and padded to the end of the room and back, looking for your dog, as they do."

"I should have smelled it."

"Probably."

"I should have heard its claws on the boards."

"One doesn't, in point of fact," said the doctor. And from the way in which he spoke, he had evidently been in the same room with a leopard and darkness by night.

"Anyway, we needn't go as far as that. The boards creaked and groaned as the temperature fell. Or, more likely still, as they imperceptibly moved back into place after your weight had rested on them."

I nodded. "Pass up."

"Next thing?"

"Something—probably not a leopard—came and played the piano."

"Recognize the tune?"

"No. There was no tune. In point of fact, it was a God Almighty (excuse me!) crash, as though some giant had suddenly struck every key in three octaves simultaneously. And so hard that some of the wires broke."

"Yes! Very disturbing in the middle of the night, and admittedly not a leopard. I'll tell you what happened."

"Thank you," said I, perhaps a shade skeptically.

"An iguana fell from a horizontal roof-beam. Full length onto, and as it happened, exactly parallel to the keyboard."

"Yes . . ." I admitted. "That would serve. Do iguanas get up in the roof?" I asked.

"Not that I know of," admitted Dr. Gates frankly. "But there's a mighty big lizard—they call it the *goh*—up here. . . ."

"What, the Siamese *toctaw?*" I asked.

"A bit bigger," said Gates. "Though I don't know that I've ever seen one that would cover three octaves on the piano. A snake could, of course," he added.

"Yes," I mused. "But it would be funny if a snake fell rigid in a straight line, like that, wouldn't it?"

"Extremely funny, except for the person who was there listening to it," admitted Gates. "But if a big snake fell ten or fifteen feet onto a keyboard of a piano, there would be some noise. Or I'll tell you what it might have been," he continued. "Not an iguana, but an ichneumon."

"Civet-cat," said I, proud of my worldly knowledge.

"Yes, same sort of thing. Now, they do inhabit roofs, and they are apt to drop most suddenly and somewhat alarmingly from the roof to the floor. It might have been an ichneumon. I had a nice little chap here, tame as a cat. Used to worry my dog frightfully, although I had taught him to accept the hitherto-wild jungle beast as a house companion. 'Tricks' was the big Airedale. Stood about a foot and a half high, and the civet-cat, Jo, used to stalk him. As Tricks walked past its hiding-place Jo would run out, climb on to Tricks's hind leg, run up and along the dog's back, and perch on his head just above his nose. I'm afraid it was the bane of poor Tricks's life, but he put up with it very patiently."

"Well, iguana, *goh, toctaw,* or ichneumon for the piano playing. Pass up. But by the way, the piano was played twice!"

"Yes, that was the iguana or *goh* scrambling off the piano, after resting, a bit winded from his fall, of course."

"Well, the next thing was an eerie shudder-making cry in the room, and an indisputable glimpse of the 'something white' of ghostly fiction. This was fact."

"Let's see," pondered the doctor. "Yes, I think we can dispose of that. There's a very large white owl in these parts, whose nocturnal habits are not blameless. He's quite equal to a sudden swoop right through your bungalow, in at the back and out at the front, uttering a shriek to curdle your blood as he does so."

"Is he intentionally offensive?"

"No—it's a —you know—'This is the house that Jack built' sort of sequence. Tiny insects such as mosquitoes and moths fly about; bats come in and catch the flying insects, and the huge white owl comes in to catch the bats. That was your ghost."

I nodded. "Pass up."

"He's rather an interesting chap, that bird. Biggest owl in the world, and the natives always attribute its cry to a *peh,* and compare the owl to the *peh-nawk.* When they hear it, they hurry inside their huts and, if possible, shut themselves in. And curiously enough, the cicadas seem to share their fear or dislike, for they always cease their shrilling, and the jungle becomes comparatively silent for some time after the cry has been heard. Some people think the cicadas shut up because they know that the owl eats them, and they realize that their natural enemy is near at hand. Anything else?"

"Anything!" I smiled. "These were only *hors d'oeuvres variés.* Yes, there was something else. . . . I fell asleep, a fact that I frankly admit, and I awoke from a dream, another fact that I frankly admit, and the dream continued for a few seconds, so to speak, as I awoke—and a rowdy party that was in my dream was continued in my room. . . . I am sure that, for a few seconds, or perhaps for part of one second, I was literally wide awake to the fact that this party was going on."

"And then?" inquired Gates.

"I found that the room was in darkness, and that the party was trooping down the steps and going in under the bungalow."

Dr. Gates eyed me steadily.

"Ah! Now you're asking for something," was the quiet reply. "But haven't you . . . ? Haven't you . . . something else to tell me?"

"Well, only that I lit my lamp, got up, pulled on my boots, and went down to investigate."

"Good for you," said Gates. "I know exactly how you felt, but what I meant was, haven't you something else to tell me about the—er—party?"

"No . . . no. . . . Oh, yes. Of course! Above the laughter and voices, I distinctly heard a crash."

"Sort of noise made by a cabinet falling down on its face?"

"Exactly."

"Yes . . . yes . . . ?"

"And then a most appalling scream. The most utterly dreadful sound I had ever heard in my life."

"Yes," agreed Dr. Gates. And I say "agreed" advisedly. For obviously he had been expecting me to say just what I had said.

"I might of course produce the *peh-nawk* to account for the scream, but I won't."

"What is it? And why not?" I asked.

"What is it? The *peh-nawk* is probably the bird I mentioned

just now. It must be a bird. Nobody has seen it, but all
jungle-dwellers have heard it. I rank myself as a jungle-dweller,
and I have heard it. Like the natives themselves, I would pay
down quite a perceptible little sum in hard cash rather than hear
it again. And I'd travel a mighty long way around a place where
it was likely to be heard. And the reason why I won't blame the
noise you heard on to the *peh-nawk* is because it wasn't made by
one."

"By what was it made then?"

"Now, my friend, you are asking another question. I will reply
with a story. A story that I think will answer that question. Also
answer the first one of the series, and that was 'Do you believe in
ghosts?' "

"Geoffrey Walsh-Kurnock built that bungalow and laid out
that plantation in that particular spot because, amongst other
considerations—climate, soil, water, labor, and so on—it was in
what he considered the Unadministered Territory. This mission
is, of course, undeniably in Unadministered Territory, and at the
moment, you are in neither China nor Burma; neither Siam nor
Cambodia. You are nowhere, in fact. Not on any map at least.

"And Geoffrey had the idea that if he made his plantation and
built his bungalow where he did, he'd be free. No one would
have any right to interfere with him.

"He was a curious chap and that was one of his
idiosyncrasies—freedom. . . . As if anyone is free—anywhere.

"However, I was glad enough when he came up this way, for it
made my nearest neighbor only sixty miles away. What one
might call quite near. One could have a monthly chat with a
fellow white man. We got along famously, with our dozen talks a
year; and, though we didn't see eye to eye on many things, we
had a mutual respect and the bond of total dissimilarity.

"He did me a lot of good, broadened my outlook, and made
me more tolerant; and I tried to do him a bit of good so far as that
was possible without being offenseive—though I must admit it

ended in my insisting on his coming and seeing me here instead of my going there, for I really am an awfully poor hand at orgy-making. I don't play cards, I don't drink and—I don't like being a wet-blanket. And whenever Geoffrey sent a messenger over, inviting me to his place for the first Saturday in the month, I knew what it meant. It meant, among other things, a wild party. For his monthly feasts became famous; and forest-officers and young teak men, wandering prospectors who had an idea that anybody who went off the beaten track was likely to stumble over large rubies, ingots of silver, or lumps of jade, elephant-hunters, and occasionally some of those wonderful people who catch large free wild beasts alive and put them in little iron cages were apt to be among his guests.

"Anyhow, a party, large or small, there always was, on the first Saturday in the month, at Walsh-Kurnock's place. Of course, it was famous, apart from hospitality, by reason of its being unique, positively the only plantation in this part of the world, the only place for hundreds of miles where a white man, or any other man, tried to grow kapok, tea, and rubber.

"Naturally it has all gone back to jungle now, and I doubt whether any of it would have done much good, unless, possibly, it was the kapok, though I have an idea that there was more in, and behind, Walsh-Kurnock than met the eye."

The doctor fell silent as he eased the tobacco in his pipe and looked extremely thoughtful.

"In what way?" I asked.

"I don't know. It was no more than wild theory on my own part, but it was such an unlikely place for such an unlikely man, that there must have been more to it than met the eye. I don't know. Oil . . . rubies . . . jade . . . silver . . . a Consular official watching Chinese encroachment from the North? And then again, it might have been just agoraphobia, just his idiosyncratic love of solitude, his yearning to escape from his fellow-man. And yet there were the wild parties . . . I don't know.

"Well, one Friday afternoon, the day before one of the monthly gatherings of half a score of people who came from all over half a score thousand square miles, Geoffrey Walsh-Kurnock was sitting on the verandah of that bungalow having tea, when there came along the track leading to the bungalow a party of Kamoo jungle-men, personally conducting a gigantic python. They do, you know, in the most extraordinary manner, something like a couple of agricultural laborers leading a bull, at home. When he thinks he'll charge to the right, the man on the left pulls him back, and when he thinks he'll charge to the left, the man on right pulls him back, and if he thinks he'll bolt straight ahead, they both pull him back.

"Same with a python. These folk tie a rattan rope around his neck, and a band of them gets at each end of it, and they lead him along. If he won't go straight ahead, they drag him. If he goes too fast, they put the brake on. If he wants to go left or right, they do exactly as the bull-leaders do.

"Perhaps you are wondering why they took the trouble to bring this great brute—over twenty-five feet long and as thick as a man's thigh—to call on Walsh-Kurnock. It was because he was assembling specimens of the fauna of this part of the world, to give, or possibly to sell, to a man who was making a collection for the American Museum of Natural History.

"So he extended a cordial welcome to what was the very finest specimen of a snake he had ever seen.

"The next problem was how to house it worthily and safely until Brooke came for it. Suddenly he remembered a packing-case in which his piano had arrived. Incidentally, just fancy a man going to the expense and trouble of getting a piano up here."

"How on earth did he do it?" I asked.

"Well, I should imagine every form of known transport was used between the warehouse in Bangkok and that bungalow; train, sampan, elephant, bullock-cart, and mostly human beast-of-burden. That piano must have come on men's heads through swamp and jungle, over hill-track and forest-path, like a stag-beetle carried by ants.

"Well, into the piano packing-case, without apology or ceremony, went the huge python, a big stone was placed on the lid, the Kamoo coolies then being handsomely rewarded with a five-satang piece—about a penny—each.

"Geoffrey returned to his tea. Nor, we may imagine, did he give the snake another thought until, at the height of the party next night, when the champagne dinner finished—it was always champagne for the guests at Geoffrey's monthly party—and the brandy-and-soda flowing, the Devil put it into somebody's mouth to say:

" 'If you drink much more, Geoff, you'll be seeing snakes.' "

"And that was what reminded him.

" 'Snakes!' he cried. 'Adam and Eve! *I'll* show you a snake! I've got the very one that escaped from the Garden of Eden, downstairs. Come and have a look.'

"And picking up the candle and telling someone else to bring the lamp, he led the way down those steps and they all trooped in under the bungalow.

" 'Here, catch hold of this,' he said to somebody, gave him the candle, went to pull the big stone off the top of the packing-case, and overturned the whole thing.

"There was a crash, as it went over and the stone and lid fell away, releasing the enormous python. Before that lot of drunken and half-drunken and wine-excited young men knew it, that twenty-five feet of immeasurable deadly strength was among them. The man holding the lamp, backing away, fell over the stone, dropping the lamp as he did so. The lamp went out. The man who held the candle fled for his life, and as the rest turned, shouting, scrambling, stumbling in the pitch darkness, bumping into the *teangs,* they heard a scream that curdled their blood.

"It was one of them who told me all this, and I shall never forget the phrase he used:

" 'It was a shrieking scream of agony and fear that seemed to rend the very fabric of the night with a gigantic tearing sound that pierced one's eardrums.'

"He wasn't an Englishman, as you may imagine.

"The first man who returned with a light held above his head saw Geoffrey Walsh-Kurnock bound to one of the twelve-foot *teangs* by a gigantic rope, a living rope, the python—whose open mouth and coldly glaring eyes hovered a few inches from those of its victim, its crushed and mangled victim, in whose body every single bone was broken a dozen times."

"Yes, I heard every detail of the whole affair from an eyewitness, the man who saw him in the serpent's coils. He came straight here, just as quickly as he could travel, and I had to nurse him for quite a while before he was fit to take up life again."

We sat awhile in silence.

"Before I leave this place, if I ever do," said Dr. Gates, "I shall come to believe that I too was an eyewitness—instead of only an earwitness—of what happened that night."

"A what?"

"An earwitness. Like yourself. The night I slept there, I heard—exactly what you did. I don't mean the creakings of the dry floor-boards nor the falling of the lizard onto the piano and the hooting of the owl; but the laughter, the descent to the place beneath, the brief hubbub, and then the cry."

"Do we believe in ghosts, you and I, Doctor?" I asked.

"No, no, of course not. Aren't we rational, sensible men? We each dreamed a dream, a nightmare, rather; and were wakened by the scream of the *peh-nawk*."

"Quite so," I agreed. "Obviously. . . . But, tell me. What was your chief essential fundamental sensation, your real mental reaction, to that bungalow?"

"Fear. Soul-shaking, mind-enfeebling, body-devitalizing *fear*," he replied.

"Mine, too," I admitted. "There I really knew fear."

The Whole Town's Sleeping

RAY BRADBURY

IT WAS A WARM SUMMER NIGHT in the middle of Illinois country. The little town was deep far away from everything, kept to itself by a river and a forest and a ravine. In the town the sidewalks were still scorched. The stores were closing and the streets were turning dark. There were two moons: a clock moon with four faces in four night directions above the solemn black courthouse, and the real moon that was slowly rising in vanilla whiteness from the dark east.

In the downtown drugstore, fans whispered in the high ceiling air. In the rococo shade of porches, invisible people sat. On the purple bricks of the summer twilight streets, children ran. Screen doors whined their springs and banged. The heat was breathing from the dry lawns and trees.

On her solitary porch, Lavinia Nebbs, aged thirty-seven, very straight and slim, sat with a tinkling lemonade in her white fingers, tapping it to her lips, waiting.

"Here I am, Lavinia."

Lavinia turned. There was Francine, at the bottom porch step, in the smell of zinnias and hibiscus. Francine was all in snow white and didn't look thirty-five.

Miss Lavinia Nebbs rose and locked her front door, leaving her lemonade glass standing empty on the porch rail. "It's a fine night for the movie."

"Where you going, ladies?" cried Grandma Hanlon from her shadowy porch across the street.

They called back through the soft ocean of darkness: "To the Elite Theater to see Harold Lloyd in *Welcome, Danger!*"

"Won't catch *me* out on no night like this," wailed Grandma Hanlon. "Not with the Lonely One strangling women. Lock myself in with my *gun!*"

Grandma's door slammed and locked.

The two maiden ladies drifted on. Lavinia felt the warm breath of the summer night shimmering off the oven-baked sidewalk. The heat pulsed under your dress and along your legs with a stealthy sense of invasion.

"Lavinia, you don't believe all that gossip about the Lonely One, do you?"

"Those women like to see their tongues dance."

"Just the same, Hattie McDollis was killed a month ago. And Roberta Ferry the month before. And now Eliza Ramsell has disappeared. . . ."

"Hattie McDollis walked off with a traveling man, I bet."

"But the others—strangled—four of them, their tongues sticking out their months, they say."

They stood upon the edge of the ravine that cut the town in two. Behind them were the lighted houses and faint radio music; ahead was deepness, moistness, fireflies, and dark.

"Maybe we shouldn't go to the movie," said Francine. "The Lonely One might follow and kill us. I don't like that ravine. Look how black, smell it, and *listen.*"

The ravine was a dynamo that never stopped running, night or day: There was a great moving hum among the secret mists and washed shales and the odors of a rank greenhouse. Always the black dynamo was humming, with green electric sparkles where fireflies hovered.

"And it won't be *me*," said Francine, "coming back through this terrible dark ravine tonight, late. It'll be you, Lavinia, you down the steps and over that rickety bridge and maybe the Lonely One standing behind a tree. I'd never have gone over to church this afternoon if I had to walk through here all alone, even in daylight."

"Bosh," said Lavinia Nebbs.

"It'll be you alone on the path, listening to your shoes, not me. And shadows. You *all alone* on the way back home. Lavinia, don't you get lonely living by yourself in that house?"

"Old maids love to live alone," said Lavinia. She pointed to a hot shadowy path. "Let's walk the short cut."

"I'm afraid."

"It's early. The Lonely One won't be out till late." Lavinia, as cool as mint ice cream, took the other woman's arm and led her down the dark winding path into cricket-warmth and frog-sound, and mosquito-delicate silence.

"Let's run," gasped Francine.

"No."

If Lavinia hadn't turned her head just then, she wouldn't have seen it. But she did turn her head, and it was there. And then Francine looked over and she saw it too, and they stood there on the path, not believing what they saw.

In the singing deep night, back among a clump of bushes— half hidden, but laid out as if she had put herself down there to enjoy the soft stars—lay Eliza Ramsell.

Francine screamed.

The woman lay as if she were floating there, her face moon-freckled, her eyes like white marble, her tongue clamped in her lips.

Lavinia felt the ravine turning like a gigantic black merry-go-

[117]

round underfoot. Francine was gasping and choking, and a long while later, Lavinia heard herself say, "We'd better get the police."

"Hold me, Lavinia, please hold me, I'm cold. Oh, I've never been so cold since winter."

Lavinia held Francine, and the policemen were all around in the ravine grass. Flashlights darted about, voices mingled, and the night grew toward eight thirty.

"It's like December, I need a sweater," said Francine, eyes shut against Lavinia's shoulder.

The policeman said, "I guess you can go now, ladies. You might drop by the station tomorrow for a little more questioning."

Lavinia and Francine walked away from the police and the delicate sheet-covered thing upon the ravine grass.

Lavinia felt her heart going loudly within her and she was cold, too, with a February cold. There were bits of sudden snow all over her flesh and the moon washed her brittle fingers whiter, and she remembered doing all the talking while Francine just sobbed.

A police voice called, "You want an escort, ladies?"

"No, we'll make it," said Lavinia, and they walked on. I can't remember anything now, she thought. I can't remember how she looked lying there, or anything. I don't believe it happened. Already I'm forgetting, I'm making myself forget.

"I've never *seen* a dead person before," said Francine.

Lavinia looked at her wristwatch, which seemed impossibly far away. "It's only eight thirty. We'll pick up Helen and get on to the show."

"The show!"

"It's what we *need*."

"Lavinia, you don't *mean* it!"

"We've got to forget this. It's not good to remember."

"But Eliza's back there now and—"

"We need to laugh. We'll go to the show as if nothing happened."

"But Eliza was once your friend, *my* friend—"

"We can't help her; we can only help ourselves forget. I insist. I won't go home and brood over it. I won't *think* of it. I'll fill my mind with everything else *but*."

They started up the side of the ravine on a stony path in the dark. They heard voices and stopped.

Below, near the creek waters, a voice was murmuring, "I am the Lonely One. I am the Lonely One. I *kill* people."

"And I'm Eliza Ramsell. Look. And I'm dead, see my tongue out my mouth. See!"

Francine shrieked. "You, there! Children, you nasty children! Get home, get out of the ravine, you hear me. Get home, get home, get home!"

The children fled from their game. The night swallowed their laughter away up the distant hills into the warm darkness.

Francine sobbed again and walked on.

"I thought you ladies'd never come!" Helen Greer rapped her foot atop her porch steps. "You're only an hour late, that's all."

"We—" started Francine.

Lavinia clutched her arm. "There was a commotion. Someone found Eliza Ramsell dead in the ravine."

Helen gasped. "Who found her?"

"We don't know."

The three maiden ladies stood in the summer night looking at one another. "I've a notion to lock myself in my house," said Helen at last.

But finally she went to fetch a sweater, and while she was gone Francine whispered frantically, "Why didn't you *tell* her?"

"Why upset her? Time enough tomorrow," replied Lavinia.

The three women moved along the street under the black trees through a town that was slamming and locking doors, pulling down windows and shades, and turning on blazing lights.

They saw eyes peering out at them from curtained windows.

How strange, thought Lavinia Nebbs, the Popsicle night, the ice-cream night with the children thrown like jackstones on the streets, now turned in behind wood and glass, the Popsicles dropped in puddles of lime and chocolate where they fell when the children were scooped indoors. Baseballs and bats lie on the unfootprinted lawns. A half-drawn white chalk hopscotch line is there on the steamed sidewalk.

"We're crazy out on a night like this," said Helen.

"Lonely One can't kill three ladies," said Lavinia. "There's safety in numbers. Besides, it's too soon. The murders come a month separated."

A shadow fell across their faces. A figure loomed. As if someone had struck an organ a terrible blow, the three women shrieked.

"*Got* you!" The man jumped from behind a tree. Rearing into the moonlight, he laughed. Leaning on the tree, he laughed again.

"Hey, I'm the Lonely One!"

"Tom Dillon!"

"Tom!"

"Tom," said Lavinia. "If you ever do a childish thing like that again, may you be riddled with bullets by mistake!"

Francine began to cry.

Tom Dillon stopped smiling. "Hey, I'm sorry."

"Haven't you heard about Eliza Ramsell?" snapped Lavinia. "She's dead, and you scaring women. You should be ashamed. Don't speak to us again."

"Aw—"

He moved to follow them.

"Stay right there, Mr. Lonely One, and scare yourself," said Lavinia. "Go see Eliza Ramsell's face and see if it's funny!" She pushed the other two on along the street of trees and stars, Francine holding a handkerchief to her face.

"Francine," pleaded Helen, "it was only a joke. Why's she crying so hard?"

"I guess we better tell you Helen. *We* found Eliza. And it wasn't pretty. And we're trying to forget. We're going to the show to help and let's not talk about it. Enough's enough. Get your ticket money ready, we're almost downtown."

The drugstore was a small pool of sluggish air which the great wooden fans stirred in tides of arnica and tonic and soda-smell out into the brick streets.

"A nickel's worth of green mint chews," said Lavinia to the druggist. His face was set and pale, like the faces they had seen on the half-empty streets. "For eating in the show," she explained, as the druggist dropped the mints into a sack with a silver shovel.

"Sure look pretty tonight," said the druggist. "You looked cool this noon, Miss Lavinia, when you was in here for chocolates. So cool and nice that someone asked after you."

"Oh?"

"You're getting popular. Man sitting at the counter"—he rustled a few more mints in the sack—"watched you walk out and he said to me, 'Say, who's *that*?' Man in a dark suit, thin pale face. 'Why, that's Lavinia Nebbs, prettiest maiden lady in town,' I said. 'Beautiful,' *he* said. 'Where's she live?' " Here the druggist paused and looked away.

"You *didn't*," wailed Francine. "You didn't give him her address, I hope? You *didn't!*"

"Sorry, guess I didn't think. I said, 'Oh, over on Park Street, you know, near the ravine.' Casual remark. But now, tonight, them finding the body. I heard a minute ago, and I suddenly thought, what've I *done!*" He handed over the package, much too full.

"You fool!" cried Francine, and tears were in her eyes.

"I'm sorry. 'Course maybe it was nothing."

"Nothing, nothing!" said Francine.

Lavinia stood with the three people looking at her, staring at her. She didn't know what or how to feel. She felt nothing—except perhaps the slightest prickle of excitement in her throat. She held out her money automatically.

"No charge for those peppermints." The druggist turned down his eyes and shuffled some papers.

"Well, I know what we're going to do right *now!*" Helen stalked out of the drug shop. "We're going right straight home. I'm not going to be part of any hunting party for you, Lavinia. That man asking for you. You're *next!* You want to be dead in that ravine?"

"It was just a man," said Lavinia slowly, eyes on the streets.

"So's Tom Dillon a man, but maybe he's the Lonely One!"

"We're all overwrought," said Lavinia reasonably. "I won't miss the movie now. If I'm the next victim, let me *be* the next victim. A lady has all too little excitement in her life, especially an old maid, a lady thirty-seven like me, so don't you mind if I enjoy it. And I'm being sensible. Stands to reason he won't be out tonight, so soon after a murder. A month from now, yes, when the police've relaxed and when he *feels* like another murder. You've got to *feel* like murdering people, you know. At least that kind of murderer does. And he's just resting up now. And anyway I'm not going home to stew in my juices."

"But Eliza's face, there in the ravine!"

"After the first look I never looked again. I didn't *drink* it in, if that's what you mean. I can see a thing and tell myself I never saw it, that's how strong *I* am. And the whole argument's silly, anyhow, because I'm not beautiful."

"Oh, but you are, Lavinia. You're the loveliest maiden lady in town, now that Eliza's—" Francine stopped. "If you'd only relaxed, you'd have been married years ago—"

"Stop sniveling, Francine. Here's the box office. You and Helen go on home. I'll sit alone and go home alone."

"Lavinia, you're crazy. We can't leave you here—"

They argued for five minutes. Helen started to walk away but came back when she saw Lavinia thump down her money for a solitary movie ticket. Helen and Francine followed her silently into the theater.

The first show was over. In the dim auditorium, as they sat in the odor of ancient brass polish, the manager appeared before the worn red velvet curtain for an announcement:

"The police have asked for an early closing tonight. So everyone can be home at a decent hour. So we're cutting our short subjects and putting on our feature film again now. The show will be over at eleven. Everyone's advised to go straight home and not linger on the streets. Our police force is pretty small and will be spread around pretty thin."

"That means us, Lavinia. *Us!*" Lavinia felt the hands tugging at her elbows on either side.

HAROLD LLOYD IN *Welcome, Danger!* said the screen in the dark.

"Lavinia," Helen whispered.

"What?"

"As we came in, a man in a dark suit, across the street, crossed over. He just came in. He just sat in the row behind us."

"Oh, Helen."

"He's right behind us *now.*"

Lavinia looked at the screen.

Helen turned slowly and glanced back. "I'm calling the manager!" she cried and leaped up. "Stop the film! Lights!"

"Helen, come back!" said Lavinia, eyes shut.

When they set down their empty soda glasses, each of the ladies had a chocolate moustache on her upper lip. They removed them with their tongues, laughing.

"You see, how *silly* it was?" said Lavinia. "All that riot for nothing. How embarrassing!"

The drugstore clock said eleven twenty-five. They had come out of the theater and the laughter and the enjoyment feeling

[123]

new. And now they were laughing at Helen and Helen was laughing at herself.

Lavinia said, "When you ran up that aisle crying 'Lights!' I thought I'd die!"

"That poor man!"

"The theater manager's brother from Racine!"

"I apologized," said Helen.

"You *see* what a panic can do?"

The great fans still whirled and whirled in the warm night air, stirring and restirring the smells of vanilla, raspberry, peppermint, and disinfectant in the drugstore.

"We shouldn't have stopped for these sodas. The police said—"

"Oh, bosh the police." Lavinia laughed. "I'm not afraid of anything. The Lonely One is a million miles away now. He won't be back for weeks, and the police'll get him then, just wait. Wasn't the film *funny!*"

The streets were clean and empty. Not a car or a truck or a person was in sight. The bright lights were still lit in the small store windows where the hot wax dummies stood. Their blank blue eyes watched as the ladies walked past them, down the night street.

"Do you suppose if we screamed they'd do anything?"

"Who?"

"The dummies, the window-people!"

"Oh, Fran*cine.*"

"Well . . ."

There were a thousand people in the windows, stiff and silent, and three people on the street, the echoes following like gunshots when they tapped their heels on the baked pavement.

A red neon sign flickered dimly, buzzing like a dying insect. They walked past it.

Baked and white, the long avenue lay ahead. Blowing and tall in a wind that touched only their leafy summits, the trees stood on either side of the three small women.

"First we'll walk you home, Francine."

"No, I'll walk *you* home."

"Don't be silly. You live the nearest. If you walked me home, you'll have to come back across the ravine alone yourself. And if so much as a leaf fell on you, you'd drop dead."

Francine said, "I can stay the night at your house. You're the *pretty* one!"

"No."

So they drifted like three prim clothes-forms over a moonlit sea of lawn and concrete and tree. To Lavinia, watching the black trees flit by, listening to the voices of her friends, the night seemed to quicken. They seemed to be running while walking slowly. Everything seemed fast, and the color of hot snow.

"Let's sing," said Lavinia.

They sang sweetly and quietly, arm in arm, not looking back. They felt the hot sidewalk cooling underfoot, moving, moving.

"Listen," said Lavinia.

They listened to the summer night, to the crickets and the far-off tone of the courthouse clock making it fifteen minutes to twelve.

"Listen."

A porch swing creaked in the dark. And there was Mr. Terle, silent, alone on his porch as they passed, having a last cigar. They could see the pink cigar fire idling to and fro.

Now the lights were going, going, gone. The little house lights and big house lights, the yellow lights and green hurricane lights, the candles and oil lamps and porch lights, and everything felt locked up in brass and iron and steel. Everything, thought Lavinia, is boxed and wrapped and shaded. She imagined the people in their moonlit beds, and their breathing in the summer night rooms, safe and together. And here we are, she thought, listening to our solitary footsteps on the baked summer evening sidewalk. And above us the lonely streetlights shining down, making a million wild shadows.

"Here's your house, Francine. Good night."

"Lavinia, Helen, stay here tonight. It's late, almost midnight now. Mrs. Murdock has an extra room. I'll make hot chocolate. It'd be ever such fun!" Francine was holding them both close to her.

"No, thanks," said Lavinia.

And Francine began to cry.

"Oh, not *again,* Francine," said Lavinia.

"I don't want you dead," sobbed Francine, the tears running straight down her cheeks. "You're so fine and nice, I want you alive. Please, oh, please."

"Francine, I didn't realize how much this has affected you. But I promise you I'll phone when I get home, right away."

"Oh, *will* you?"

"And tell you I'm safe, yes. And tomorrow we'll have a picnic lunch at Electric Park, all right? With ham sandwiches I'll make myself. How's that? You'll see; I'm going to live forever!"

"You'll phone?"

"I promised, didn't I?"

"Good night, good night!" Francine was gone behind her door, locked tight in an instant.

"Now," said Lavinia to Helen. "I'll walk *you* home."

The courthouse clock struck the hour. The sounds went across a town that was empty, emptier than it had ever been before. Over empty streets and empty lots and empty lawns the sound went.

"Ten, eleven, twelve," counted Lavinia, with Helen on her arm.

"Don't you feel *funny?*" asked Helen.

"How do you mean?"

"When you think of us being out here on the sidewalk, under the trees, and all those people safe behind locked doors lying in their beds. We're practically the only walking people out in the open in a thousand miles, I bet." The sound of the deep, warm, dark ravine came near.

In a minute they stood before Helen's house, looking at each other for a long time. The wind blew the odor of cut grass and wet lilacs between them. The moon was high in a sky that was beginning to cloud over. "I don't suppose it's any use asking you to stay, Lavinia?"

"I'll be going on."

"Sometimes . . ."

"Sometimes what?"

"Sometimes I think people *want* to die. You've certainly acted odd all evening."

"I'm just not afraid," said Lavina. "And I'm curious, I suppose. And I'm using my head. Logically, the Lonely One can't be around. The police and all."

"*Our* police? *Our* little old force? They're home in bed too, the covers up over their ears."

"Let's just say I'm enjoying myself, precariously but safely. If there were any *real* chance of anything happening to me, I'd stay here with you, you can be sure of that."

"Maybe your subconscious doesn't want you to live anymore."

"You and Francine, honestly."

"I feel so guilty. I'll be drinking hot coffee just as you reach the ravine bottom and walk on the bridge in the dark."

Lavinia Nebbs walked down the midnight street, down the late summer night silence. She saw the houses with their dark windows and far away she heard a dog barking. In five minutes, she thought, I'll be safe home. In five minutes I'll be phoning silly little Francine. I'll—

She heard a man's voice singing far away among the trees.

She walked a little faster.

Coming down the street toward her in the dimming moonlight was a man. He was walking casually.

I can run and knock on one of these doors, thought Lavinia. If necessary.

The man was singing, "Shine On, Harvest Moon," and he carried a long club in his hand. "Well, look who's here! What a time of night for you to be out, Miss Nebbs!"

"Officer Kennedy!"

And that's who it was, of course—Officer Kennedy on his beat.

"I'd better see you home."

"Never mind, I'll make it."

"But you live across the ravine."

Yes, she thought, but I won't walk the ravine with *any* man. How do I know *who* the Lonely One is? "No, thanks," she said.

"I'll wait right here then," he said. "If you need help give a yell. I'll come running."

She went on, leaving him under a light humming to himself, alone.

Here I am, she thought.

The ravine.

She stood on the top of the one hundred and thirteen steps down the steep, brambled bank that led across the creaking bridge one hundred yards and up through the black hills to Park Street. And only one lantern to see by. Three minutes from now, she thought, I'll be putting my key in my house door. Nothing can happen in just one hundred and eighty seconds.

She started down the dark green steps into the deep ravine night.

"One, two, three, four, five, six, seven, eight, nine steps," she whispered.

She felt she was running but she was not running.

"Fifteen, sixteen, seventeen, eighteen, nineteen steps," she counted aloud.

"One-fifth of the way!" she announced to herself.

The ravine was deep, deep and black, black. And the world was gone, the world of safe people in bed. The locked doors, the town, the drugstore, the theater, the lights, everything was gone. Only the ravine existed and lived, black and huge about her.

"Nothing's happened, has it? No one around, is there? Twenty-four, twenty-five steps. Remember that old ghost story you told each other when you were children?"

She listened to her feet on the steps.

"The story about the dark man coming in your house and you upstairs in bed. And now he's at the *first* step coming up to your room. Now he's at the second step. Now he's at the third and the fourth and the fifth step! Oh, how you laughed and screamed at that story! And now the horrid dark man is at the twelfth step, opening your door, and now he's standing by your bed. 'I *got you!*' "

She screamed. It was like nothing she had ever heard, that scream. She had never screamed that loud in her life. Her heart exploded in her. The sound of its terrified beating filled the universe.

"There, there!" she screamed out loud to herself. "At the bottom of the steps. A man, under the light! No, now he's gone! He was *waiting* there!"

She listened.

Silence. The bridge was empty.

Nothing, she thought, holding her heart. Nothing. Fool. That story I told myself. How silly. What shall I do?

Her heartbeats faded.

Shall I call the officer, did he hear my scream? Or was it only loud to *me?* Was it really just a small scream after all?

She listened. Nothing. Nothing.

I'll go back to Helen's and sleep the night. But even while she thought this, she moved down again. No, it's nearer home how. Thirty-eight, thirty-nine steps, careful, don't fall. Oh, I *am* a fool. Forty steps. Forty-one. Almost halfway now. She froze again.

"Wait," she told herself. She took a step.

There was an echo.

She took another step. Another echo—just a fraction of a moment later.

"Someone's following me," she whispered to the ravine, to the black crickets and dark green frogs and the black steam. "Someone's on the steps behind me. I don't dare turn around."

Another step, another echo.

Every time I take a step, *they* take one.

A step and an echo.

Weakly she asked of the ravine, "Officer Kennedy? Is that *you?*"

The crickets were suddenly still. The crickets were listening. The night was listening to *her*. For a moment, all of the far summer night meadows and close summer night trees were suspending motion. Leaf, shrub, star, and meadow grass had ceased their particular tremors and were listening to Lavinia Nebbs' heart. And perhaps a thousand miles away, across locomotive-lonely country, in an empty way station a lonely night traveler reading a dim newspaper under a naked light bulb might raise his head, listen, and think, What's that! and decide, Only a woodchuck, surely, beating a hollow log. But it was Lavinia Nebbs, it was most surely the heart of Lavinia Nebbs.

Faster. Faster. She went down the steps.

Run!

She heard music. In a mad way, a silly way, she heard the huge surge of music that pounded at her, and she realized as she ran—as she ran in panic and terror—that some part of her mind was dramatizing, borrowing from the turbulent score of some private film. The music was rushing and plunging her faster, faster, plummeting and scurrying, down and down into the pit of the ravine!

"Only a little way," she prayed. "One hundred ten, eleven, twelve, thriteen steps! The bottom! Now, run! Across the bridge!"

She spoke to her legs, her arms, her body, her terror; she advised all parts of herself in this white and terrible instant. Over the roaring creek waters, on the hollow, swaying, almost-alive bridge planks she ran, followed by the wild footsteps behind, with the music following too, the music shrieking and babbling!

"He's following. Don't turn, don't look—if you see him, you'll not be able to move! You'll be frightened, you'll freeze! Just run, run, *run!*

She ran across the bridge.

Oh, God! God, please, please let me get up the hill! Now up, up the path, now between the hills. Oh, God, it's dark, and everything so far away! If I screamed now it wouldn't help; I can't scream anyway! Here's the top of the path, here's the street. Thank God I wore my low-heeled shoes. I can run, I can run! Oh, God, please let me be safe! If I get home safe I'll never go out alone. I was a fool, let me admit it, a fool! I didn't know what terror was. I wouldn't let myself think, but if you let me get home from this I'll never go out without Helen or Francine again! Across the street now!

She crossed the street and rushed up the sidewalk.

Oh, God, the porch! My house!

In the middle of her running, she saw the empty lemonade glass where she had left it hours before, in the good, easy, lazy time, left it on the railing. She wished she were back in that time now, drinking from it, the night still young and not begun.

"Oh, please, please, give me time to get inside and lock the door and I'll be safe!"

She heard her clumsy feet on the porch, felt her hands scrabbling and ripping at the lock with the key. She heard her heart. She heard her inner voice shrieking.

The key fitted.

"Unlock the door, quick, quick!"

The door opened.

"Now inside. *Slam* it!"

She slammed the door.

"Now lock it, bar it, lock it!" she cried wretchedly. "Lock it *tight!*"

The door was locked and barred and bolted.

The music stopped.

She listened to her heart again and the sound of it diminishing into silence.

Home. Oh, safe at home. Safe, safe and safe at home! She slumped against the door. Safe, safe. Listen. Not a sound. Safe, safe, oh, thank God, safe at home. I'll never go out at night again. Safe, oh safe, safe, home, so good, so good, safe. Safe inside, the door locked. *Wait.* Look out the window.

She looked. She gazed out the window for a full half minute.

"Why there's no one there at all! Nobody! There was no one following me at all. Nobody running after me." She caught her breath and almost laughed at herself. "It stands to reason. If a man *had* been following me, he'd have *caught* me. I'm not a fast runner. There's no one on the porch or in the yard. How silly of me. I wasn't running from anything except me. That ravine was safer than safe. Just the same, though, it's nice to be home. Home's the really good warm safe place, the *only* place to be."

She put her hand out to the light switch and stopped.

"What?" she asked. "What? *What?*"

Behind her, in the black living room, someone cleared his throat. . . .

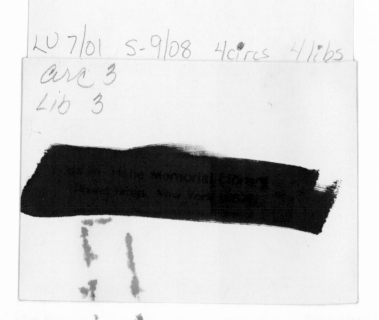